MONTANA MAVERICKS

Welcome to Big Sky Country, home of the Montana Mavericks! Where free-spirited men and women discover love on the range.

THE ANNIVERSARY GIFT

The mayor of Bronco and his wife have invited the whole town to help celebrate their thirtieth anniversary, but when the pearl necklace the mayor bought his wife goes missing at the party, it sets off a chain of events that brings together some of Bronco's most unexpected couples. Call it coincidence, call it fate—or call it what it is: the power of true love to win over the hardest cowboy hearts!

Rylee Parker had a crush on Shep Dalton all through high school, but she knew it would never go anywhere. So when he offers to make good on their childhood pledge to marry each other if they're still single by thirty, she knows he's kidding. He has to be—right? But what starts as a joke soon gets out of hand, and if she's not careful, they could wind up walking down the aisle for real!

Dear Reader,

When my editor offered me the chance to write a Montana Mavericks book (my very first!), I was so excited that I barely slept that night. I grew up reading Harlequin books, and the Montana Mavericks continuity is a beloved classic.

I'm so honored to be able to tell you Shep Dalton and Rylee Parker's story, which is about two childhood friends finding each other again years later. The spark they shared as kids will ignite into a romance that neither one of them can deny. But when they revisit a promise made in their teen years, it's not just their love that will hang in the balance—their future together will, too.

I hope you enjoy this trip to Montana, where the romance is as big and beautiful as the sky overhead! And for more information about me, my books and for the occasional fun giveaway, follow me at Facebook.com/kaylienewell.

Happy reading!

Kaylie Newell

THE MAVERICK'S MARRIAGE DEAL

KAYLIE NEWELL

Special thanks and acknowledgment are given to Kaylie Newell for her contribution to the Montana Mavericks: The Anniversary Gift miniseries.

✦ HARLEQUIN®

ISBN-13: 978-1-335-59476-1

The Maverick's Marriage Deal

Copyright © 2024 by Harlequin Enterprises ULC

Recycling programs for this product may not exist in your area.

For questions and comments about the quality of this book, please contact us at CustomerService@Harlequin.com.

® is a trademark of Harlequin Enterprises ULC.

Harlequin Enterprises ULC
22 Adelaide St. West, 41st Floor
Toronto, Ontario M5H 4E3, Canada
www.Harlequin.com

Printed in Lithuania

MIX
Paper | Supporting responsible forestry
FSC® C021394

For **Kaylie Newell**, storytelling is in the blood. Growing up the daughter of two writers, she knew eventually she'd want to follow in their footsteps. She's now the proud author of over twenty books, including the RITA® Award finalists *Christmas at the Graff* and *Tanner's Promise*.

Kaylie lives in Southern Oregon with her husband, two daughters, a blind Doberman and two indifferent cats. Visit Kaylie at Facebook.com/kaylienewell.

Books by Kaylie Newell

Montana Mavericks: The Anniversary Gift

The Maverick's Marriage Deal

Harlequin Special Edition

Sisters of Christmas Bay

Their Sweet Coastal Reunion
Their All-Star Summer
Their Christmas Resolution

Visit the Author Profile page
at Harlequin.com for more titles.

For Matt. Happy twenty-five years. I love you.

Chapter One

Shep Dalton held the small present in his hand and glanced around. The room was packed. Actually, packed was an understatement. Everywhere he looked there were people—drinks in their hands, laughing and talking underneath balloons and streamers and two giant disco balls that tossed chaotic twinkles of light over them like confetti. Over the top, but not surprising. His old high-school classmate Janet Halstead, the birthday girl, was one of the first of his friends to turn thirty, and Janet had always leaned toward being a little extra. So, disco balls? Absolutely.

Shep didn't mind though. This party had gotten him away from the ranch in Bronco on the very same day they were worming and inoculating the cattle, which meant he was in a good mood. In fact, he was ready for a beer or two.

Adjusting his Stetson over his eyes, he scanned the room for the gift table. He needed to deposit this thing and find Janet and her husband, Frank, to say hello. He hadn't seen her since she'd moved to Wonderstone Ridge. Frank was well-off and had connections, which was why he'd been able to rent this place out for the party. The Wonderstone Ridge Indoor Theme Park and Aquarium. Quite a mouthful, but it was quite a place. It had been under construction for a while and hadn't even officially opened yet, so this event was a big deal. The entire county had been wanting to get a look inside for months. Now, thanks to Janet, her friends and family, at least, were getting their wish.

Narrowing his eyes, he spotted what looked like the gift table not too far from a floor-to-ceiling aquarium full of tropical fish. The table was overflowing, of course, and topped with a fancy-looking, three-tiered cake.

Muttering his apologies and touching the brim of his Stetson, he brushed past a group of twentysomething women drinking champagne and giggling at who knew what.

"Don't be sorry, cowboy," a pretty brunette said, giving him a wink as he walked by. "I'm not."

Shep smiled but didn't stop. She was wearing a huge rock on her ring finger that was hard to miss. In fact, most of the people here seemed to have shown up with their better halves. He guessed that was what happened when you were nearing thirty. Marriage, kids, a house with a white picket fence that was mortgaged to the hilt. Maybe that was generalizing, but it sure seemed accurate from where he stood. And all of a sudden, he felt like a damn fish out of water surrounded by all these happy couples.

"Shep Dalton? Is that you?"

Looking up, he saw Janet making her way toward him, weaving gracefully in between her guests. She wore a silver sequined dress that sparkled and flashed, and was giving the disco balls above her a run for their money.

He grinned. It was good to see her. He'd always liked Janet, who was obviously living the dream, complete with three adorable kids. At least, according to her Facebook pictures.

"I was hoping you'd come," she said, standing on her tiptoes to kiss him on the cheek. "But I know how hard it is to tear you away from that ranch."

"Happy birthday, Janet. I wouldn't have missed it."

"It's been a long time." She pulled away and smiled, rubbing her lipstick from his jaw. "Handsome as ever, I see. When are you going to settle down with some lucky lady?"

A distinctive warmth crept up his neck. *Here we go.* What was so wrong with being single, anyway? Janet sounded exactly like his mother, who couldn't wait to marry him off, just like his brothers. Still, even as he thought it, he remembered a promise he'd made years ago. And remembered the girl he'd made it to as well.

He cleared his throat. "This is a good turnout. You always knew how to throw a party."

She laughed, looking around. "Yes, well. A lot of these people are Frank's business associates, so I don't even know them that well. He saw an excuse to schmooze and took it. But some friends from high school came, so that makes me happy."

"Oh yeah?" A waiter walked by with a tray of champagne glasses, and Shep grabbed one with a nod. He'd never been much for champagne, but when in Rome... He took a sip, the bubbles fizzing on his tongue. "Who showed up from high school?"

"Oh, my old cheerleading friends. Anna Delgado from the drama club—remember her? She moved away from Tenacity about the same time I did. She lives up north and just had a baby." Janet tapped her lips with a manicured index finger. "Who else… *Oh!* Rylee Parker is here. You should be happy about that. You two were thick as thieves."

Shep had been taking another sip of champagne, but at the sound of Rylee's name, he swallowed with some difficulty.

"Rylee's here?" he managed.

"She was over by the aquarium, the last I saw her." Janet gazed up at him. "You know, I was always kind of surprised you two didn't end up together. You would've made a cute couple."

Shep's gut tightened at that. Nobody in his small hometown of Tenacity had known how he'd felt about Rylee back then. Least of all Rylee. But Janet was right about one thing—they *had* been thick as thieves. Which probably wasn't the right way to put it because the most trouble they'd ever gotten into was skipping class to go swimming in the river every now and then. And he'd had to twist her arm to do that. Rylee had always been a little shy, a great student, definitely a rule follower. Despite Shep trying to corrupt her in the best way possible.

Thinking about her now, he felt his lips stretch into a smile. He winked down at Janet, wanting to keep her guessing. Maybe this party was going to be more interesting than he'd thought.

"You never know, Janet," he said.

Her delicate eyebrows rose at that. "Well, what—"

She didn't finish her sentence because an older woman appeared out of nowhere and tapped her on the shoulder.

"Janet, honey, the caterer has a question about the crab cakes. I wasn't sure what to tell her."

"Oh, thank you, Linda. I'll be right there." She turned

to Shep again and pointed to his chest. "Don't think we're done with this conversation, mister."

He nodded. Then watched her make her way toward the presumed crab cake problem as the thumping music overhead changed to something softer.

Looking down at the drink in his hand, he frowned. So, he was going to see Rylee again. With her auburn hair and those beautiful blue eyes. He imagined her on the banks of the river all those years ago, the water droplets on her shoulders sparkling like diamonds. He'd felt so protective of her back then. She was too good for him. Too good for anyone, as far as he was concerned.

Nope. Champagne wasn't going to cut it. He definitely needed a beer.

Rylee took a sip of her champagne and wrinkled her nose. She hated champagne. It always gave her heartburn. But that was Rylee in a nutshell. Not exactly super comfortable at parties like this.

Actually, scratch that. She didn't *used* to be comfortable at parties like this. But that was before. Before she'd grown into a confident, capable, educated woman with an MBA who also happened to be the recently named director of marketing for the Bronco Convention Center.

She swallowed hard. If she had to repeat it over and over again, that's exactly what she'd do. Even though her days of being the shy, studious type were long behind her now, that little girl tried to resurface sometimes, which was inconvenient at best.

Gazing at the colorful fish making circles in the aquarium, she took a deep breath. She'd stay until Janet cut her cake, and then she'd head home. Aside from a few high-school acquaintances, she really didn't know anyone here, and there was a pint of Ben & Jerry's mint chocolate-chip ice cream with her name on it back at her apartment.

She took another sip of champagne, not letting herself think too much about the fact that leaving a party to go chow down on ice cream at home was *exactly* what a shy, studious type would do.

"Well, if it isn't my old swimming buddy…"

Startled, she turned at the sound of the gravelly voice behind her.

And then she stood there, unable to say anything at all. Her heart beat like a drum as she stared up at the handsome cowboy in the red plaid shirt a few feet away. He was grinning at her. A familiar, mischievous sparkle in his blue eyes.

Shep Dalton…

She could hardly believe it. It had been so long since she'd seen him that she had to blink to make sure she wasn't imagining this. Of course, she shouldn't be surprised. He'd been friends with Janet, too. And thanks to the local grapevine, she knew he lived in Bronco as well. His family had moved a few years ago after his father had gotten lucky at the slots in Las Vegas. They now owned a sprawling ranch in Bronco Heights called Dalton's Grange.

Still, she'd never run into him in town, even though she'd expected to these last few years.

She felt her lips tilt into a smile, warmth spreading across her chest. It was the way he was looking at her. It was the same way he'd looked at her in high school—like she was different from all the other girls. At least, that was how he'd always made her feel. Not that Shep would be remotely interested in someone like her. Rylee knew that without a doubt. He was much too spirited and adventurous. He always had been.

"Shep?" she managed.

"The one and only."

He stepped forward and wrapped her in a bear hug. Then lifted her completely off the ground until she laughed breathlessly.

Setting her down again, he pushed his off-white Stetson up on his forehead and grinned down at her.

"It's been a long time, Rylee," he said. "I don't think I would've recognized you if Janet hadn't told me you were here."

She touched her hair. "Do I look that different?"

"Just more mature," he said. "That's all. But still pretty as a picture."

Her cheeks heated. She'd always nursed a terrible crush on Shep for this exact reason.

"You're still a charmer, Shep."

He leaned against the wall and put his hands in his jeans pockets. His shirt stretched over his broad shoulders, and it wasn't too hard to imagine what he looked like without it. Shep was a rancher, after all, and his body was long and lean. Muscular from working long hours outdoors.

Rylee's throat felt dry all of a sudden, and she shifted on her feet. She could still smell his scent from when he'd wrapped her in his arms a minute ago. Musky, leathery. Very, very male.

"So," he said. "Tell me everything. What have you been up to? I haven't seen you since you left for college. That's a long time to be going to the river by myself."

She smiled. "I don't believe for one second that you've been too lonely without me."

"Maybe, maybe not. But you were always my favorite swimming partner. Nobody ever came close after you left."

She leaned against the wall, too, watching him. It wasn't difficult to watch Shep Dalton. He was fairly easy on the eyes. He looked pretty much the same as the last time she'd seen him, that day she'd come to say goodbye before leaving Tenacity for college. Except his face was a little more weathered now. There were sexy crinkles around his eyes, and his skin was a deep, golden tan— another nice result of working outside all day.

"I heard you'd moved to Bronco," she said. "I've been meaning to look you up, but you know. Work, life… I'm always so busy."

"What do you do?"

"Chuck Carter recently promoted me to the marketing director for the Bronco Convention Center."

He raised his eyebrows. "Impressive."

"Well, since Geoff Burris and the Hawkins Sisters are such big rodeo stars, there are a lot more opportunities now to expand." She smiled. "What about you? Still working the ranch?"

He nodded. "Yes, ma'am, and the last of my brothers to get married or engaged. Much to my mother's dismay."

"She's trying to get you to settle down?"

"They're *all* trying to get me to settle down. I mean, is it just me, or is it some kind of law around here to be married by thirty?"

At that, her heartbeat slowed a little. Twelve years might've passed since she'd seen her old childhood friend and crush, but she remembered their promise like it had been made yesterday. *If we're not married by the time we're thirty...*

She took another sip of champagne. Either it was starting to make her dizzy or Shep was.

He smiled slowly, gazing down at her. "You remember, don't you?"

"Remember what?"

"You know what."

"I have no idea what you're talking about."

"Liar."

She laughed, unable to help it. "Shep, that was a long time ago."

"It was, but I'm not married. And I haven't heard you mention a significant other, either."

"So?"

"*So...* A promise is a promise."

She sipped her champagne again. Definitely dizzy. "Let's change the subject."

"To what?"

She looked around, desperate for something else to talk about other than their promise to marry each other by the time they turned thirty. Never mind that she was twenty-nine now. And three-quarters.

She supposed she didn't want to talk about it because it hit too close to home. When they'd made that vow, Shep might've made it lightheartedly, but she hadn't. The thought of marrying him back then had warmed her blood, and then some.

"Janet's probably getting ready to cut her cake," she said awkwardly. "And open her presents. I got her a coffeemaker..."

He nodded, looking amused. She couldn't blame him. It wasn't exactly a smooth transition.

"What did you get her?" she asked, plowing on, feeling her face burn.

"A necklace."

"A necklace?" *Oh dear.* Her coffeemaker was going to pale in comparison. "What kind of necklace?"

"A strand of pearls. They reminded me of something Janet would wear. I picked them up at a vintage store in Bronco."

Rylee nodded, chewing her bottom lip. Something about that nagged at her, but she didn't know why. *A strand of pearls...* And then it hit her. The mayor had bought his wife a strand of pearls for their thirtieth anniversary back in January and infamously, it had disappeared right after. She remembered the description that went out locally, along with a press release begging for them to be returned. In fact, she still had a picture of the pearls on her phone.

She fished it out of her purse and pulled the photo up while Shep watched curiously.

"Do you remember that necklace of Mayor Smith's that went missing a few months ago?" she asked. "He put an ad in the newspaper and on the radio station, asking for people to keep an eye out?"

"Vaguely. Why?"

She held the picture up and showed him. "Does the necklace you bought Janet look anything like this?" The pearls had a delicate gold clasp with a tiny rose embossed on it. A sweet touch, and something that would set it apart from other necklaces, but only if you were looking hard enough.

Frowning, he studied the enlarged image. "Actually… that looks exactly like it."

"Oh no. If it's the same one, someone could've stolen it and then pawned it."

"Great." Shep craned his neck to look across the room. "It's the same. I'm sure of it. And I just put it on the gift table. We should go snatch it back before anyone notices. I can't give her a stolen necklace."

Rylee's pulse skipped in her wrist. "Poor Janet. We have to steal her present back?"

"Before anyone notices. Are you up for it?"

Shep's eyes sparkled. She recognized that look. This was exactly the kind of thing the two of them would've done all those years ago. Dared each other on a whim. And then they'd dissolve into ridiculous fits of laughter afterward.

"Come on," he said. "The mayor will be thrilled."

"His wife will be, too."

"Janet, not so much."

"But what she doesn't know won't hurt her, so…"

"That's what I'm thinking," Shep said. "What do you say, partner?"

Rylee looked around quickly, feeling seventeen again. Apparently, this was what Shep was going to do to her. Make her feel like a teenager again. With all the wild emotions that went along with it.

He reached out and took her hand. Heat immediately shot up her arm and into her heart. His grip was warm and solid, making her feel safe, just like it used to. Like all her insecurities were nonexistent, and it was just the two of them against the world.

"Stick close," he said. "I'll make sure nobody sees."

* * *

Shep led Rylee through the crowded room, holding her hand firmly in his. It felt good holding her hand, familiar and natural. He remembered holding it years ago, when they'd jump off their favorite rock into their secret swimming hole in the river. Back then, he'd been able to talk Rylee into almost anything. But he'd never put her in jeopardy, ever. He'd cared too much about her for that.

He looked over his shoulder now, struck again by how lovely she was in her dark-wash jeans and sparkly pink sweater. She'd only gotten lovelier over the years, something he wouldn't have thought possible before. He'd found himself wanting to tell her that a few minutes ago when they'd been talking by the aquarium, but he'd stopped himself twice. He didn't know what was wrong with him. He normally wasn't so starstruck by women. In fact, they were usually the ones affected by him—or so he'd been told. But Rylee… Rylee had always been different. Special. But he didn't need to go embarrassing himself now by gushing about how good it was to see her again.

Instead, he squeezed her hand as they weaved their way toward the gift table. He could hardly believe the necklace he'd bought for Janet had ended up being stolen property. Definitely a bad look to be giving it as a present. Thank God Rylee had said something in time.

She pressed herself against him, her body warm against his back. "Who's going to be doing the swiping?" she whisper-yelled. He could barely hear her over the music overhead. "You or me?"

He turned to her, leaning close. He could smell her perfume, something flowery and sweet. "One of us will have to swipe. The other one has to be the lookout."

"I don't want to be the swiper. I'll be the lookout."

"Fair enough."

"I think we need a backup plan in case someone sees us."

"We'll just say I forgot to put the card with it or something," he said. "That's believable."

"Talk about a mission impossible."

"Maybe not impossible. But definitely a mission awkward."

She laughed, like she might be enjoying this a little. Which wasn't so weird, because he was, too. He'd had a few beers by now, which were definitely making him less inhibited than he would've been otherwise. He rubbed his thumb along the back of her hand, struck by how soft her skin was. Like satin.

"You ready?" he asked. "I'm counting on the lights from the disco balls distracting everyone."

She laughed again. He'd been right. She was clearly enjoying this, which made his gut tighten.

"I'm ready."

"Okay," he said. "Cover me."

He made his way to the gift table, hoping he looked inconspicuous enough. If anyone did see him swiping the present, he'd have to explain, and the thought of that made him cringe.

He sneaked a glance at Rylee, and she gave a quick thumbs-up. Apparently, the coast was clear. It was now or never.

Looking back at the gift table, which was significantly fuller now than when he'd left it earlier, he spotted the little box next to a few brightly colored gift bags. Maybe this would be easier than he'd thought. All he had to do was sidle up to it and snatch it back with nobody seeing.

Slowly, he stepped up to the table and took a deep breath. But when he looked over at Rylee again, she suddenly shook her head.

"Can you believe all those presents?"

Shep turned to see an older man standing there holding a glass of wine and looking a little unsteady on his feet. The lights from the disco balls flashed on his bald head.

Shep smiled. Probably too widely. He'd almost been caught in the act.

"Right?" he said. He could feel Rylee watching from across the room. "A lot of presents, for sure."

"Once my wife gets a load of this," the other man said with a hiccup, "she'll want a party like this next year. Who can afford it? Renting out an entire aquarium?" He shook his head, as if he'd been waiting to get this off his chest since walking through the door.

Shep nodded and watched as the man finally meandered off.

He looked back at Rylee, who gave him another thumbs-up. Before he could second-guess himself, he stepped close to the gift table again, grabbed the present and shoved it behind his back. Probably looking guilty as sin, but whatever. At least he'd gotten it back.

Grinning widely, Rylee motioned him over.

"Can you put it in your purse?" he asked, walking up to her. "Otherwise, it'll have to go down the back of my jeans, and that's just wrong."

She laughed. "Sure. I'll take it back to the mayor this week. He'll be so happy."

"Mission accomplished, partner."

"We do make good partners, don't we?"

"We absolutely do."

"It makes me think of when we were kids..." She let her voice trail off and looked away, as if suddenly embarrassed.

"What's wrong?"

"Nothing. It just brings up old memories. It wasn't always easy growing up in Tenacity, was it?"

He frowned. That was the understatement of the century. Tenacity was a blue-collar town. Full of hardworking people, ranchers mostly, who barely scraped by. Shep's home life had been hard: his parents' marriage was rocky; his dad cheated... And Rylee's childhood had been difficult sometimes, too. A surprise baby and the youngest sibling of three older brothers, she'd felt lonely and isolated growing up. She'd always been close with her mom, but her dad had been strict and stubborn, and not always the easiest to get along with.

As neighbors, he and Rylee had been close because they'd had so much in common. Mainly wanting to leave Tenacity for greener pastures as soon as they could manage it. She and Shep had both gone to college, but he'd stayed local. Rylee had gone out of state, excelling in her university classes, just like she'd excelled in high school.

And now, here she was. Very grown, very beautiful, obviously a success. She'd made something of herself, just like he'd known she would. Yet he could still see traces of that girl underneath. A little shy, a little sad. It was hard shaking your past. He should know. He'd been trying to shake his for years. Trying to wiggle out from underneath his father's questionable shadow. Attempting to convince folks in Bronco that his family was more than just their "new money." But that was how everyone always treated them. They hadn't exactly been welcomed to town with open arms.

Suddenly, that sweet, vulnerable look on Rylee's face made him want to wrap her in his arms. More than that, it made him want to kiss her.

She gazed up at him, her eyes impossibly wide and dark. Maybe it was the beer, but he didn't think so. There was more going on here than just the alcohol flowing through his veins. There was a distinctive heat growing between them that was hard to deny.

Her gaze dropped to his mouth. And then, before he could think about it, he leaned down and pressed his lips to hers.

Chapter Two

Rylee thought her knees were going to give out. Or her heart. She could hardly believe that Shep was kissing her, and more than that, she was kissing him back. Eagerly.

All thoughts of whether or not people would see (which, of course they would, since she and Shep were standing in the middle of the room) entered her mind fleetingly and then left like a sigh on the breeze. Right then, she simply didn't care. She just wanted him closer. To be kissing him longer, deeper.

He wrapped a strong arm around her waist and pulled her close. His body was solid and lean, warm against hers. His lips were soft, but insistent. His scent, that musky, leathery scent that she'd caught earlier when he'd hugged her, enveloped her senses and made her stomach curl into a tight little ball. She'd imagined kissing Shep plenty when she was a teenager, but never in her wildest dreams had she known it would be this good. That *he* would be this good.

From somewhere distant, she realized that people were clapping. And whistling.

Her eyes fluttered open at the sound.

Slowly, Shep broke the kiss. Then pulled away and looked around.

Sure enough, there was a half circle of people standing there smiling at them. Obviously happy to see a young couple in love. Or what they thought was a young couple in love.

Rylee touched her tingling lips, her face flushed.

Shep cleared his throat. "Just giving my new fiancée a kiss," he told the crowd with a wink.

Rylee gaped up at him as a collective *aww* moved through the room.

"What are you *doing*?" she whispered.

He leaned close to her ear. "Having some fun. Everyone else here seems to be married or engaged. Why shouldn't we?"

"Nobody's going to believe we're actually engaged, Shep."

"Why not?"

"For one thing, I'm not your type. Clearly."

"Isn't that the other way around?"

She stared up at him. Before she could answer that, a woman walked up and patted Rylee on the shoulder.

"Well, congratulations, you two," she said.

Shep beamed at her. "Thank you."

"Uh…thank you?" Rylee said. Shep had come up with some wild ideas when they were kids, but this took the cake. *Engaged?*

Still, even at that thought, she couldn't deny the warm feeling spreading through her body as he rested his hand on her lower back. Protectively. A little possessively, and what woman in her right mind wouldn't want to be possessed by Shep Dalton?

When they were alone again, Rylee turned to face him

square on. His cowboy hat bathed his face in shadow. He looked like a rugged hero out of an old Western.

"What do you think you're doing?" she asked, planting her hands on her hips.

"I'm sorry. I should've asked before I kissed you. That would've been the gentlemanly thing to do."

"Well, I kissed you right back. But that's not what I'm talking about."

He smiled, two long dimples cutting into each scruffy cheek.

"Shep…"

"Okay," he said. "I'll admit I got caught up in the moment. This party, everyone here. All our friends and family getting married, and there's so much pressure to do the same. But honestly, what can it hurt? We just play along for the night, and we get to see what all the fuss is about."

She shook her head, but the look on his face, that playful, youthful look, was so familiar that she could feel it whittling away at all her sensible excuses.

"Aren't you just a *little* tempted to play along?" he asked.

He had to know she was. Her heart had swelled to twice its size when that nice lady had walked up to congratulate them just now. And when everyone had clapped at their kiss? She'd loved that feeling, too. Happiness. Pride. Excitement. All of it. It was *very* tempting to pretend that she was Shep's fiancée. At least for a few harmless hours.

"Maybe a little," she said, looking down at her shoes.

He touched her chin with his fingertips, until she looked up at him again.

"A little?"

"Okay. I'm tempted."

He smiled. "Fun, right?"

She smiled, too. They'd always had fun together. Climbing trees, swimming in the river, riding their bikes. And the trouble they'd gotten into? It had sustained her when she'd felt the loneliest of her whole life. Shep had a way of making her feel vibrant and colorful. Adventurous and spirited, just like he was. He'd always rubbed off on her, and he was rubbing off on her now. Not such a terrible thing, when she thought about it. There were worse things than feeling vibrant and colorful.

"Fun," she said.

And meant it.

"I guess I had more to drink than I thought," Rylee said, touching her temple.

They were standing in the small motel lobby, waiting for the front desk lady to run Shep's card.

"I know," he said. "Me, too. Staying the night is definitely the right call. We can't drive back to Bronco like this."

It was true, they couldn't. But he also wasn't hating the idea of spending the night with Rylee, either. Even if they'd gotten the last room available, and it only had one bed, which meant he'd be sleeping on the sofa.

That was okay. He simply wasn't ready for the night to be over with yet. Pretending to be engaged to Rylee had proven even more entertaining than he'd thought. They'd spent the rest of their time at the party dancing, laughing and getting hearty congratulations from Janet's guests. Not to mention having a few more drinks, which had eventually landed them here. The Mountain Summit Motel, which was right across the street from the aquarium. A good thing, since Shep's head was way too fuzzy to drive.

He smiled down at the lady checking them in, and she smiled back, handing him the key card and telling them where the ice machine was.

"Y'all have a good evening," she said.

Shep nodded and followed Rylee out the door into the early April night. Stars sparkled overhead, and the air was chilly against his skin. He could hear semis passing on the highway at the edge of town, but beyond that, the shadowy mountains loomed in the distance, where he knew the Montana evening would be alive with the sounds of nature.

Rylee looked up at the stars, her silky hair falling past her shoulders.

"Can you believe how many of them there are?" she said.

He looked up, too. "I know. It makes you feel small, doesn't it?"

"It really does."

"Did you miss Montana?" he asked, turning to her again. "When you left for college?"

She smiled, her lips looking soft and painfully kissable. "California is great," she said. "And it'll always have a special place in my heart, but yes. I missed Montana."

"I used to think about leaving, too," he said after a minute. "But when Dad bought the ranch in Bronco, he talked my brothers and me into coming to work it. We didn't want to. But my mom had just had a heart attack, so we wanted to make her happy..."

Rylee frowned, gazing up at him. "Oh no. Is she okay?"

"She's okay now, but it was touch and go for a while

there. It forced some perspective on all of us. Especially my dad. You know how rocky their marriage was…"

"I remember."

"But they've worked things out. I think it helped that we stayed together as a family. Dalton's Grange has kept us close."

"I'm sure you're right."

He shrugged. "So, here I am. I'll probably always be a rancher, and that's okay. It's in my blood. But sometimes I wonder what it would've been like to leave. Like you did."

"But I came back…"

"That you did."

They began walking down the motel's breezeway, toward their room at the end. A peaceful silence settled between them, and Shep had to work not to put his arm around her. Despite having kissed her like a teenage boy tonight, and pretending that they were engaged to boot, they actually weren't even a couple. In fact, there was a reason why Shep hadn't settled down like his brothers. He'd never taken relationships seriously. And to be completely honest, calling them relationships was generous. Shep had flings. Flings with the same type of women over and over again—pretty women, women who were more interested in landing themselves a wealthy cowboy than anything else.

Up until this point, they were exactly his type though, because they hadn't required anything more from him than some charm on dates and some skill in bed. He'd been able to protect himself from falling for anyone, because there'd never been anyone worth falling for.

But here, now, walking with Rylee underneath the lights of the motel breezeway, there was a sudden desire for more. He had no idea what *more* meant, but the feeling was definitely there. Something that was trying to fill some kind of emptiness inside him.

Whatever this was that he and Rylee had going right now, it was delicate, and he didn't want to mess it up by kissing her again or making her feel uncomfortable whatsoever. Which meant keeping his hands to himself. And absolutely keeping his lips to himself.

"I think this is us," she said, pointing to the last door on their right.

He pulled the key card from his back pocket and unlocked the door. Flipping on the light, he looked around. The room was small, clean, simple. But just like the front-desk lady had said, there was only one bed. A queen with a print of a mountain lake over the headboard.

Rylee looked over at him.

"It's okay," he said. "I'll take the couch."

"It's too small, you'll never fit."

"I've slept on worse."

"Shep…"

"The couch it is."

She tossed her purse on the bed. "Well. You're a gentleman."

"Don't let it get around."

"I'm exhausted," she said, stifling a yawn.

"Me, too. I'm not used to dancing like that."

"I haven't danced like that *ever*. But it was fun, right?"

"It was fun."

He smiled at her, and she smiled back. For a minute, they were quiet, just looking at each other. Shep's chest tightened as his gaze dropped to her mouth. That *very* kissable mouth, and he had to force himself to look away before he said something, or did something, to embarrass himself. He was still buzzed and didn't trust his own judgment. At all.

"I don't suppose we're going to talk about that kiss," she said, sinking down on the bed and taking off her shoes. "I mean, we probably should, right?"

He walked over and sat on the couch, bouncing on it a few times to test it out. It was lumpy, but he'd live. His biggest problem was going to be not thinking about Rylee in that bed with her jeans off. He imagined her soft, milky-white legs moving underneath the crisp sheets, and his throat tightened.

He took his Stetson off and put it on the end table with a sigh. It was going to be a long night.

"I have to be honest," he said. "I don't regret it."

"Kissing me?"

"Hell no. Why would I?"

"Well…" She frowned, seeming to contemplate this. "What about the complications?"

"What complications?"

"Feelings…you know."

"I can see how that might happen. But at the moment, the only feeling I'm having is being worried I'll do it again."

She smiled.

He took off his boots and stretched out on the couch. His legs hung all the way off the end. Hooking his elbow behind his head, he eyed his feet dangling past the armrest.

She curled up on the bed and turned to face him with her pillow underneath her cheek. She looked so pretty that all of a sudden he couldn't believe she was actually single. Men had to be lining up for Rylee. Why in the world was she still on the market and pretending to be engaged to *him*?

"What?" she asked. "What are you thinking?"

"I'm just wondering how it is that you're not married. Or spoken for."

She wrinkled her nose. "Oh. Well, I was. Once upon a time. Not married, but engaged. He broke it off right before the wedding. So, I haven't exactly been lucky in love."

"I'm sorry," he said. "That couldn't have been easy."

"It wasn't. It took me a long time to get over it. And now I've got some trust issues that I'm working through. You know the drill."

He really didn't, as he'd never committed to anyone in the first place. He used to tell himself he wasn't interested in commitment, and maybe that had been true when he was younger. But lately, he had to admit there was some fear there, too. Fear of turning out just like his father, who'd been a dismal example of a husband most of his adult life.

"What about you?" she asked. "Have you ever gotten close to marriage?"

He shook his head. "Nah. I don't think I'm the marrying type."

"I doubt that. You just haven't met the right person yet. It'll happen, and when it does, you'll know."

"Never say never. I mean, I went from being single to engaged in about two minutes flat tonight, so there's that."

"Oh my God," she said, slapping a hand over her eyes. "I completely forgot about that. How did I forget about that?"

"The champagne."

She readjusted the pillow underneath her head. "Shep. What if people in Bronco find out? My parents and your parents? What if word gets around that we said we're engaged? I mean, it's bound to."

He thought about that. Actually, it was the first time he'd stopped to think about it the entire night. Which was exactly like him. He didn't usually make a habit out of looking before he leaped. But the problem was, this time he'd leaped with Rylee alongside him.

He scraped a hand through his hair. "Maybe not. I mean, Wonderstone Ridge isn't right next door to Bronco or anything."

"But what about Janet?"

"I think she's got her hands full with her own life. She might be curious… Okay, she'll be curious for sure, but we did a good job of steering clear of her after the whole engagement announcement thing. I know she was a little tipsy, just like we were. She might forget all about it by morning."

He knew this was stretching it, but he didn't want Rylee to worry. The truth was, though, that news traveled fast in towns like Bronco and Wonderstone Ridge. The chances of people hearing about this were fairly decent. He'd have to admit it was all a joke, and by then his poor mother would know about it. She was so desperate to have him settled down, it would be a shock to her system.

Across the room, Rylee was deep in thought and nibbling on her bottom lip, which wasn't doing anything for his willpower. He'd already been having a hard enough time not imagining her half naked, and now this.

"I think I'm gonna take a shower," he said. *A cold shower.* "Unless you need the bathroom first?"

"No, that's okay. I'll wash my face when you're done."

Sitting up, he rolled his head from side to side until his neck cracked. Yup. It was going to be a long night.

Rylee couldn't sleep. She kept staring up at the motel room ceiling, listening to the soft sound of Shep's breathing a few feet away.

He'd come out of the bathroom earlier in his jeans and nothing else. When she realized she was staring, she turned into her pillow, trying to pretend she was drowsy.

He'd flopped down on the couch with a groan, and after a few minutes, she'd gotten up to use the bathroom and wash her face. But she'd been picturing him shirtless ever since.

Shep had always been blessed with good looks. When he was a teenager, all the girls in their high school had crushes on him, and Rylee, of course, had been no exception. He was a rancher, through and through, but he reminded her now of the boys she'd met in California. The ones with the sun-kissed skin and the messy blond hair. Always looking like they'd just come back from surfing or spending the day at the beach. But none of those boys could hold a candle to Shep Dalton, or his rock-hard abs. Or those broad shoulders and thick biceps. *Or* that teasing smile that made her want to melt into a puddle on the floor.

She rolled over for what must've been the tenth time in a matter of minutes, her heart thrumming in her chest. When he'd taken his Stetson off earlier, she'd had the ridiculous urge to cross the room and run her hands through his hair, through the ring his hat left behind. It was so tempting that she'd had to bite her cheek just to distract her dumb ovaries.

He sighed, and she wondered with a pang of guilt if he was uncomfortable on the couch. He'd looked so funny earlier, with his feet hanging off the end. He'd have to be scrunched up now. How was he supposed to sleep that way?

She could hear him shifting back and forth, trying to get settled. The couch creaked and popped under his weight, and she finally sat up to face him in the dim light of the room.

"Shep," she said. "There's no way you can be comfortable on that thing."

"I'm okay…just finding the right position."

"There is no right position," she said. "Why don't you just sleep in the bed with me?"

He was quiet at that, and all of a sudden, her face warmed. He probably thought she was coming on to him. But could she blame him? It sounded like some kind of line. Some kind of cheesy way to get him into bed. Literally.

"I mean…if you want to," she said. "You don't have to. I just thought you'd be able to sleep better over here."

"Well, I'd be more comfortable for sure. But I'm not sure I'd sleep any better."

Rylee could feel her pulse skipping in her throat. This was *so* unlike her. She clearly remembered a time, back when she and Tyler had been together, when she'd been too shy to come out of the bathroom in a skimpy nightie that he'd bought her. And now, here she was, inviting her old childhood crush into bed with her. Sure, she hadn't been planning on jumping his bones, but he didn't know that.

"Are you sure?" Shep asked.

She gave a quick nod. Then realized he couldn't see her

in the dark. "I'm sure," she said, forcing an evenness into her voice that she didn't feel. "We'll behave ourselves."

After a minute, he pushed himself off the couch and walked over to the bed, his muscular body dark and imposing in the shadowy room.

He pulled back the covers and climbed inside, and she could immediately smell his scent. That incredibly erotic scent from earlier tonight that gave her butterflies now.

He plumped the pillow underneath his head and turned on his side to face her. This close, she could clearly see him smiling. Maybe even see that teasing twinkle in his eyes. But she could be imagining that part.

"Thanks for sharing," he said. "My legs were starting to cramp up."

She laughed, pulling the covers up around her shoulders. The bed felt warmer with him in it. Her body *definitely* felt warmer.

"I'm surprised you lasted as long as you did," she said. "That couch is tiny, and you're not exactly a small guy."

"I know. I went through some weird growth spurt after high school. The good news is that most of my brothers have to look up at me now, so that's a plus."

"How are your brothers? Other than married off?"

"They're doing pretty well. Dale is the only one who isn't married yet, but he's engaged. He's also going to be a stepdad. Mila is eight and adorable. Morgan's also got a daughter, Josie, who's three."

Rylee could hardly believe the boys she remembered so well were family men now. But then again, she couldn't believe she and Shep were almost thirty, either. It seemed like just yesterday that they were sneaking to the river together.

"How about your brothers?" he asked. "How are they doing?"

She swallowed hard. Her family was a touchy subject for her these days. The truth was, her older brothers, all in their early thirties, had had a tumultuous relationship with their father for as long as she could remember. Living on the ranch hadn't been easy for them. Braden and Miles had finally left Tenacity, following in Hayes's footsteps, who'd been the first to go. He'd broken up with his girlfriend, Chrissy Hastings, crushing her heart in the process, and had left years ago, never looking back. It was still a sore spot in their family, an open wound that hadn't healed.

"They're okay," she said quietly. "They moved away. We talk, but I don't get to see them very much, which makes me sad. But living with my dad just got to be too much for them. You know how he is."

Shep nodded somberly.

She was sure he remembered her family's complicated dynamics. Her father loved his kids, but he was notorious for being hard on them. They couldn't be good at something; they had to be the best. Something that Rylee had struggled with plenty. Her brothers struggled with it, too. Maybe even more so, since they were the ones their dad expected to take over the ranch someday, and the ranch was everything to their father.

"And how are your parents?" Shep asked.

"They're doing pretty well. I keep trying to get them to come visit, but Dad doesn't like to leave the ranch very often, and Mom doesn't like to leave him. So it's this whole thing. I try to get back when I can, but honestly, it isn't enough. I feel guilty about that, but I just had to leave when I got the chance, you know?"

Shep sighed. "I know what you mean. Tenacity was a hard place to grow up. But it's full of good people. Honestly, I miss it sometimes."

She let that settle. Shep's family was well-off now. He didn't have to worry anymore about all the things that had plagued them as kids. The things that had bonded them from the beginning.

"From Tenacity to Bronco," she said softly. "And not just Bronco Valley, either. Bronco *Heights*. That's quite a change."

"It is. The Daltons are finally getting to see how the other half lives."

"I'd love to get out to your ranch someday…"

"I'd love to show it to you. Do you still ride?"

Rylee smiled against her pillow. As a kid, she'd had an old gelding named Tuff that she and Shep used to ride bareback. He was the best horse in the world. But since she'd moved from her family's ranch, she only rode periodically now.

"Not as often as I'd like," she said.

"Well, we might have to fix that. I have a pretty Appaloosa that you'd look awfully good on. Just saying."

They lay there quiet for another few seconds, just watching each other. Then suddenly, without warning, Shep reached out and brushed a lock of hair away from her eyes. His touch was so soft, so tender, that her heart just about stopped in her chest.

"I've missed you, Rylee," he said, his voice low. "I'm sorry I never kept in touch."

She swallowed hard. His fingertips left a tingling trail

along her skin. She still couldn't believe she was lying here next to him. If anyone had told her this morning that this was how her evening would end up, she would've laughed at the absurdity of it. But here she was.

"I've missed you, too," she said. "You were my best friend. I'm not sure what I would've done without you all those years."

"Let's make each other a promise."

"Uh-oh. I've heard that before."

He smiled. "This one doesn't involve getting married. Or pretending that we're going to get married."

"Okay, then. I'm game."

"Let's not fall out of touch again. No matter what happens, okay?"

She smiled, too. She was finding it nearly impossible not to smile when she was this close to him. He had that effect.

"I promise," she said softly. "Cross my heart."

Chapter Three

Rylee sat across from Shep in the little booth with the red checked tablecloth and opened her menu. The spring sunshine was out in force this morning, shining in through the diner window in long shafts of warm gold. It felt good on her shoulders, even better on her cheeks. She hadn't slept much last night and resisted another yawn as she read through the breakfast items, which looked heavenly.

"Do you still like waffles?" Shep asked. He had a way of reading her mind. An unsettling thought, since her mind had been full of nothing but him for the last sixteen hours or so.

"I *love* waffles," she said. "But they don't love my thighs, unfortunately. I'm trying to cut down on sugar."

"That's no fun. Plus, I think your thighs are perfect as is."

She smiled, lowering her lashes. He said that like she was sexy, beautiful. When she knew very well she wasn't either of those things. She was pretty enough, and that was fine. She'd always been okay with that. There was much more to life than looks, but she had to admit, it was nice feeling beautiful. In fact, she could get used to it, and that worried her a little.

"What about you?" she asked. "What sounds good?"

"I think I'm gonna have the cheese omelet with a side of bacon." He patted his nonexistent belly. "Gotta fuel up for today."

"What's happening today?"

"The rest of the cattle inoculations. I'm sure my brothers are a little pissed that I wasn't there to help yesterday."

"And that you didn't come home last night."

"None of their business. But I'm sure there will be questions. There are *always* questions."

She nodded. She got it. Sometimes it seemed like she was her brothers' favorite topic of conversation. Who she was dating, who she wasn't. What her life (or love life) looked like in general. They never let up, always wanting to insert themselves where they weren't needed. But that was the problem—they still thought she was a little girl. Overly protective and assuming they were needed constantly.

Her phone buzzed from her purse, and she pulled it out to see a text from her best friend, Gabrielle Hammond, flash across the screen.

Her stomach dropped. *Shoot.* She'd forgotten to let her know how the party was, and she never forgot to text Gabby. She'd be worried, probably thinking Rylee had ended up in a ditch somewhere. Even though they'd only known each other a relatively short amount of time (Gabby and her little girl, Bella, were fairly new in town), they'd hit it off, and were more like sisters now than anything else.

"Everything okay?" Shep asked.

"Yup. It's just my friend Gabby. I was supposed to check in last night, and I kind of went radio silent."

"Uh-oh."

"Do you mind if I answer this really quick?"

"Go for it."

Rylee sat back and opened Gabby's message.

Girl, I went for coffee this morning, and I ran into Tessa McAlister, who used to live on the second floor at BH247 (Remember her? She's got the cute little wiener dog?), and she said her brother went to Janet Halstead's birthday party last night, and that he saw you and Shep Dalton there, and that you two are ENGAGED??? Text me back, or I'm gonna have to come find you.

Rylee blinked at her phone, hardly able to believe what she'd just read. All of a sudden, the thought of food turned her stomach.

"I don't like that look," Shep said, leaning forward. "What's wrong?"

"You're not going to believe this, but Gabby wants to know why she just heard that we're engaged."

He stared at her, his blue eyes wide. "What?"

"Yeah. We thought word traveled fast in Bronco, but it's more like lightning speed. What are we going to do?"

He rubbed the back of his neck. "I'll fix it. Don't worry. I got you into this, I'll get you out."

Rylee looked back down at her phone and typed out a quick reply to Gabby. Something that would tide her over, with a little groveling thrown in for good measure. This was definitely something she'd have to explain in person.

After a minute, she tucked her phone back in her purse and set her elbows on the table.

"The easiest thing would just be to come clean, right?" she asked. "I mean, that makes the most sense."

"Right. We'll have to explain ourselves and take some ribbing, but it won't be too bad."

She chewed the inside of her cheek. She had to admit, despite everything, there was a part of her that hated to see this end. Last night was so fun, twirling around that dance floor in Shep's arms, having him hold her in front of everyone, like she was his, and he was hers. It had almost been like a dream come true. At least, for the teenage girl inside her.

Shep took a sip of his coffee and set it down with a sigh. "I have to admit though, hypothetically, it would've been nice having my mom off my case for a while. She means well, she really does, but she's been driving me nuts about getting married. Having a family. All of it."

Rylee watched him, her heart beating steadily inside her chest.

"Hmm," he said.

"Hmm, what?"

"I just had a crazy thought."

"*You?* Never."

He smiled that old mischievous Shep Dalton smile, and her belly curled.

"What if we kept it up for a while?" he asked slowly.

She stared at him.

"I mean, *technically*, we could tell people we're engaged," he continued. "We've known each other forever, so that wouldn't be too much of a stretch. Definitely fast, but nothing unheard of. Then, after a few weeks, we could fake break up." He shrugged. "That way my family would give me a relationship breather, and we wouldn't have to come right out and admit that we led everyone astray at Janet's party. Win, win."

She grew still as the words sunk in. There were all kinds of reasons to say no to this. It was wild, even by Shep's standards. But she could also see reasons to say yes, too. And yeah, okay, getting to pretend to be engaged to him was at the top of that list. But this also might be a way to get her brothers to come home again. She'd be willing to bet they might if they got news she was going to be married. And having everyone under the same roof together was almost too tempting to pass up. Of course, she'd eventually have to tell them the wedding (or fake wedding) was off, but by then maybe her family would be on their way to some kind of reconciliation. It could happen. Anything could happen.

She felt her lips tilt into a smile. "Partners in crime. I guess old habits die hard."

"There *would* be a fair amount of acting involved, though," he said. "I mean, we'd have to make it look believable. At least, when we're out in public."

He didn't have to know she was looking forward to that part. And not just a little, either. If she wasn't actually going to marry Shep Dalton, she could at least pretend she was going to marry him, and that was a close second.

"I don't have a problem with that," she said evenly, somehow managing to sound almost nonchalant about the whole thing. Who said she couldn't act? "I'm up for it if you are."

He smiled again. And there was an unmistakable twinkle in his eyes.

Rylee's pulse quickened accordingly. There was a time when that look had set her heart on fire. This morning, a whole decade later, she found that nothing much had changed. Her heart was still burning for Shep Dalton and those impossibly blue eyes.

She took a sip of her iced tea, hoping it would cool her off some. So, they were going to be engaged for a few weeks. At least as far as Bronco, Montana, was concerned.

She just hoped she and her burning heart could take the heat.

Shep flipped his truck's sun visor down as he made his way along the newly paved drive that led to Dalton's Grange. He could see the ranch house in the distance, a sprawling two-story log mansion that reminded him of something out of an epic western. It wasn't his taste, but his parents had loved it immediately, so he kept his mouth shut. Their ranch in Tenacity had been more his style. A smaller, lived-in home, and a one-hundred-year-old barn that sat up on the hill overlooking the pastures.

Dalton's Grange was much fancier. The fencing along the property alone was worth more than their old house. The barn was state of the art, with room for all the family's horses, plus some boarders. It was a nice spread, an expensive spread, but Shep thought it was ostentatious. He felt like people in Bronco thought the Daltons were tacky with their Las Vegas money, and this place definitely didn't help.

He rubbed the scruff on his chin. Spending last night with Rylee had him in the strangest mood. Reflecting on his childhood and all the insecurities he'd had as a teenager. Growing up in a family that was complicated at best, stormy at worst, Shep hadn't made a habit of confiding in friends back then. Rylee was the only one, and it hadn't taken long to fall right back into that old place with her.

Talking into the early hours of the morning and for two more hours over breakfast, when they'd decided about how to move forward with this fake engagement.

He guessed he should probably feel like he was in over his head. Like they should come clean before the whole thing got out of hand. But he felt exactly the opposite. Calm and collected for the first time in months. For one thing, he knew his mother would be happy about this. Sure, she'd be upset when he and Rylee "broke up" in a few weeks, but for the time being, it would give him a break from the constant relationship nagging. And when the time came to break the news that they were no longer together, he'd let his mom down gently. It would be fine. She'd be fine.

But what really had Shep invested in this was the fact that he was going to get to spend so much time with Rylee. And not just that, he'd be pretending to be her man. Childish? Maybe. But ever since they'd fleshed out the details this morning, his heart had been pounding strong and sure inside his chest. His gut had been tight, anticipating getting to hold her again. Maybe even getting to kiss her again, in front of anyone curious and watching. It was like getting to be in an amazing relationship, but bypassing all the crap leading up to it—getting to know someone, being nervous around them, worrying where it was going and how fast. With Rylee, all those things had already been addressed or didn't apply anyway. And the bonus? He was crazy attracted to her. This was just going to be fun. Period. Ever since he'd run into her last night, that was the word that kept reverberating in his head.

He pulled his truck into the big, circular drive and came to a stop next to his dad's Mustang. A fire-engine red midlife crisis that his mother had just signed off on. "As long as he doesn't drive into a tree, I'm okay with it," she'd said with a shrug. His mom was a saint.

He put the truck into Park and killed the engine, looking up to see his older brother Boone making his way down the house's front porch steps.

Shep took a deep breath and braced himself. Boone had that look on his face. That look that said Shep was in trouble. Probably for skipping out on the cattle branding and inoculating yesterday, but honestly, he'd do it all over again if he had the chance.

Opening his truck door, he climbed out as Boone stalked up to him.

"Where the hell have you been?" his brother asked, his brown Stetson pulled low over his eyes. Boone was a big guy. Thick through the shoulders and a little taller than Shep—the only brother who was.

"I told you. I had that party in Wonderstone Ridge last night. Can't help it if your memory has slipped with your old age." Shep closed the door and jingled his keys in his hand.

"You're only four years younger than me, smart-ass."

"Yeah, but apparently, much younger cognitively."

"Since when do you stay overnight at parties?"

Boone was watching him closely. The news about Rylee was going to come out sooner rather than later (in fact, Shep was surprised Boone hadn't already heard), but he didn't feel like going into it right then, so he stepped around his brother and made a beeline for the house. He was going to have to change clothes before heading out to the pasture and fielding the rest of Boone's questions. And probably his father's, too.

"I smell bacon," he said over his shoulder. "Did you save me some?"

"Go ahead," Boone called after him. "Run away. I'll find out what you were up to, little brother. I always do."

Ignoring that, Shep took the porch steps two by two. He wasn't really hungry after that breakfast with Rylee, but he'd needed to change the subject.

He opened the front door and stepped inside, letting the screen door slam behind him. Taking his Stetson off, he took a deep breath. He definitely smelled bacon.

"Shep?" his mother called from the kitchen. "Is that you?"

"Yup, just heading upstairs to change."

He was the only one of his brothers who lived in the main house. His room was set apart from the others and felt pretty private, so it was alright for now. Besides, he worked so much, he really only slept there anyway.

"Will you come in here, please? Right now?"

Shep stopped in his tracks. *Uh-oh.* He didn't like that tone. He wondered if she'd heard the gossip already. If Rylee's best friend knew, there was a good chance his mother did, too.

Slowly, he headed into the kitchen, his boots thudding on the hardwood floor.

Deborah Dalton was standing at the sink, drying her cast-iron skillet with a blue checked towel. She turned with a smile, looking pretty this morning. Her cheeks were rosy, and her blue eyes were bright. Her dark blond hair was pulled into a ponytail at the nape of her neck, making her look younger than her sixty-two years.

Shep leaned against the wall, waiting, but he already knew what was coming. He could tell. It didn't matter if he wasn't in the mood to tell the entire story, he was going to have to tell it anyway.

Warmth crept up his neck and into his face, making him feel like a kid who'd just been caught with his hand in the cookie jar.

His mom set the skillet down and tossed the towel on the counter. Then planted her hands on her hips.

"Is there something you want to tell me, son?"

"Um…"

"You might as well just come out with it, Shepard."

For some reason, he hadn't expected this part would be so hard. What if she could see right through him? What if she thought he was absolutely nuts for getting engaged this fast? What if he couldn't pull this off? Then what? Talk about digging himself into a hole.

"Well—"

"Rylee *Parker*?" his mother interrupted with a grin. "I didn't even know you two were dating!"

He had to stop himself before an automatic *we're not* escaped his mouth.

"It's kind of a long story," he said, feeling the first pangs of guilt for lying to her. He had to remember this was only temporary, that it would all be over soon enough. In the meantime, he'd get a little breather, and that was the whole point. Well, that and getting to kiss Rylee again.

His mother pulled out a chair at the kitchen table and motioned for him to do the same. "I have time," she said cheerfully. "And the cattle can wait."

"Tell that to Boone."

"He'll live. But I might not if I don't get some information out of you right this minute. Now *sit*."

Shep did as he was told, settling back against the chair.

His mom continued watching him closely, as if he were about to pull a rabbit out of his Stetson or something. He wasn't sure how it was possible, but maybe he'd underestimated how badly she wanted him to get married.

"You know Rylee is living in Bronco now," he began evenly.

She nodded.

"Well, we ran into each other, and one thing led to another, and we just kind of…picked up where we left off." At least that part wasn't a lie. He resisted the urge to loosen his collar.

"Oh, how romantic," his mom said, clasping her hands in front of her chest. "And you just popped the question? That's so spontaneous of you! I had no idea you had those kinds of romantic impulses, Shep. None at all."

He swallowed hard. "I'm sorry, Mom. It took me by surprise, too." Something else that was true. Maybe this wasn't going to be so bad after all.

"It's all right. I'm just so happy for you. You know I've been hoping for this all along."

"I know."

"So, when are you going to bring her out to see us? It's been so long. I don't think I've seen her since you two were in high school."

Shep shifted in his chair. His mother would want to make a special dinner. It would be a thing. He'd need to give Rylee plenty of notice, so she'd be prepared for the family onslaught.

"Uh…"

"How about next Saturday?"

"Next Saturday?"

"I'll make spaghetti and meatballs. Does she like spaghetti?"

He had no clue if she liked spaghetti. Or meatballs.

"I'll just plan on spaghetti," she said. "And if she'd like something else, I'll make that instead. I'm just so excited about this, honey."

"Thanks, Mom."

"I suppose I should give her parents a call. Wow, I don't think we've seen Norma and Lionel since we moved to Bronco."

"No," Shep said quickly. "I mean, I don't even know if she's had a chance to talk to them yet. You should probably wait on that."

"Okay. Whatever you say."

She smiled, looking for the most part like he'd just made her entire millennium. He was going straight to hell.

"Do your brothers know?" she asked.

"No…"

"When are you going to tell them?"

"Soon."

"Well, don't wait too long, Shep. You don't want them hearing from someone else like I did."

He frowned. "Who *did* you hear it from?"

"Janet's mother. She's in my old quilting group from Tenacity."

Shep resisted the urge to slap his forehead. *Of course.* He'd forgotten about the infamous quilting group, the fastest way to get word around the great state of Montana and then some.

"Anyway," she continued. "Make sure you tell them. I'll tell your father."

He forced a smile. That was going to be the messy part

of this engagement ruse. The best part would be seeing Rylee again.

He just hoped she was having a better time of it across town than he was.

Rylee sat on Gabby's couch, holding her little girl, Bella, on her lap. She leaned forward and breathed in the freshly shampooed scent of Bella's silky brown hair as the toddler thumbed through a picture book in quiet fascination.

In the kitchen, Gabby was making them each a cup of coffee, which Rylee needed desperately. She'd been planning on telling Gabby the whole truth, but now, sitting here, she wondered if it might be better to fib, at least for the time being. Bella might overhear their conversation, and that would complicate things. Even though she was only two, she could repeat something. It had happened before. And then there was the fact that Gabby would want to tell Ryan Taylor, her fiancé. Rylee didn't feel right asking her to keep this from him. If she didn't know, that would alleviate that problem right there. Sure, Gabby would be more than annoyed when Rylee ended up telling her the truth, but at this point, it was a calculated risk. She just wished she'd had more time to think this through. She still couldn't believe how fast Gabby had heard about Shep.

"Shoot," Gabby said, holding the fridge door open and frowning at the contents. "We're out of cream. Will milk do?"

"Of course," Rylee said. "Your coffee is delicious even without the cream."

"I don't know about that, but I'm getting better at it.

Ryan is a coffee fanatic, so since Bella and I moved in, I've been getting lots of practice. Elsie, *no!*"

Rylee swallowed a laugh as Gabby shoved her little dog gently aside with her foot. Elsie's favorite activity was sticking her nose into the refrigerator. She was a chunk and seemed to be getting fatter by the day. Gabby had a theory that it was because of all the food Bella dropped on the floor, but Rylee thought Elsie just liked to eat. Who could blame her?

"Here we go," Gabby said, walking over with two steaming cups of coffee. "Bella, honey, why don't I turn on *The Wiggles* for you so Rylee and Mommy can talk, okay?"

She didn't have to ask twice. Bella ran over to the television set and plopped down cross-legged on the carpet. "Ready, Mama," she said, giving an adorable thumbs-up.

Gabby turned on the TV with the volume down low and sat next to Rylee.

Rylee took a sip of her coffee and burned her tongue. Frowning, she set the mug on the coffee table. She was nervous, and she was never nervous around Gabby. She hoped her friend wouldn't notice.

"So," Gabby said with a knowing look. "Tell me everything."

"Well…you remember me talking about Shep Dalton, right?"

"Of course. Your best friend from when you were kids."

Rylee nodded and licked the taste of coffee from her lips. "We ran into each other not long ago, and one thing led to another…" She cringed inwardly. Technically, last night would count as *not long ago*, but really. What a whopper.

"One thing led to another," Gabby repeated evenly. "Meaning your engagement?"

Rylee nodded again, avoiding her friend's gaze.

"And you didn't tell me?" Gabby asked.

"It all happened so fast. And I knew you'd understand…" Rylee swallowed hard. Gabby might understand now, but would she when the truth came out? It was a lot to ask. Even for a friend as true as Gabby.

"Okay, I guess I forgive you. But for now, I just want details. Like where's your ring?"

"Oh…uh…" Rylee glanced down at her hand. "I don't have one yet. It happened—"

"I know. It happened so fast. And you're happy, Ry? *Really* happy?"

Rylee took a deep breath. At least she didn't have to fib about that part.

"I am," she said softly.

Elsie jumped up on the couch, gave Rylee a lick on the hand and curled into a little ball by her side.

"So, you're happy," Gabby said. "And now we need to plan for your *wedding*."

"No way. You're the one talking about getting married this summer."

Gabby waved her away. "Please. We can plan together. There must be something in the water, right?"

"I know. What are the odds that we could be getting married so close together?"

"Not just us. Winona Cobbs and Stanley Sanchez finally set a wedding date."

"They have? Oh, that makes me happy."

"Me, too. They really prove that it's never too late to fall in love."

Rylee smiled. Winona Cobbs, Bronco's most famous psychic (and some would say eccentric), was in her nineties. She and Stanley gave Rylee hope that happily-ever-after really did exist in the real world. Gabby was right. It was never too late.

"So," Gabby said, "when do Ryan and I get to meet Shep?"

There was an excited look in Gabby's eyes that made Rylee feel all kinds of guilty. But as she glanced over at Bella, she knew not telling her had been the right call. The little girl was hanging on their every word.

"Who's Ship, Mommy?" Bella asked, her long bangs hanging over one eye.

"Shep, honey. And he's Rylee's fiancé. That means they're going to get married. Isn't that fun?"

If Bella understood what marriage was, she didn't let on. "Can I have Goldfish?" she asked.

"In a minute, sweetie."

"But I'm *hungry*, Mama."

"Just a minute, Bella." Gabby gave Rylee a look. "She's cranky. It's past her nap time."

"I need to get going, anyway. I have to pick up some groceries and stop by the pharmacy before they close. I can never get that done during the week."

That was true, she did have to do those things, but this conversation with Gabby was only highlighting the fact that she needed to call her parents and let them know about Shep, like *now*. They were going to hear about it any day now. She'd already waited too long to say something. She was just going to have to bite the bullet, and this was as good a time as any. She'd give them a call as soon as she got into her car, while she still had the nerve.

"How's the new position, by the way? I'm *so* proud of you," Gabby said.

"It's great. Just busy, but in marketing, that's always a good thing."

They talked about Rylee's marketing plans for upcoming events at the convention center for a minute, then Gabby asked, "Is Geoff Burris still in Europe?"

Bronco's beloved rodeo star and his fiancée, Stephanie, were out of the country, but that didn't mean Rylee could take a breather. The other Burris brothers and the Hawkins Sisters kept the convention center on its toes and Bronco's rodeo fans on the edge of their seats.

"He is. Enjoying the good life for a while." Rylee looked at her watch. She really should get going, so poor little Bella could get a nap. "Thanks for the coffee. It was delicious, as usual. Call you later?"

"Okay. But don't think you're off the hook with this engagement story. You haven't even scratched the surface yet, Rylee Parker. And tell Shep we want to meet him. Your bestie has final approval."

Rylee laughed and leaned over to give her friend a hug. "I'll let him know. You'll like him, I promise." Even as she said it, though, she worried about keeping up this pretense in front of friends and family. A room full of strangers was one thing. People who knew and loved her and Shep was something else altogether.

Grabbing her keys from the coffee table, she said a little prayer that her acting chops would be good enough. And that pretending to be engaged to Shep Dalton would be worth the heartache in the end.

Rylee sat in her little car as it idled at the curb in front of Ryan and Gabby's house. She'd dialed her mother as soon as she'd climbed in, just like she'd planned. But this conversation was proving even harder than she'd thought, and she'd known it wouldn't be easy.

She stared out the window to the mountains in the distance, and listened to the heavy silence on the other end of the line.

"Mom?" she said. "Say something."

Her mother exhaled slowly. "I'm just digesting this, honey. It's kind of a surprise, that's all."

Rylee's belly sank at that. She felt so *guilty*. But she swallowed hard and told herself to power through. This was only temporary, right?

"I know," she said. "I'm sorry it's such a shock. But it's Shep. You know Shep."

"Yes," her mother said, as if she were choosing her words carefully. "We do. But you two haven't seen each other in ages, Rylee."

"We haven't. But we've always had such a strong connection. It was easy taking this step."

"Right. But it's fast."

"It is." There was no use arguing with that, since it was absolutely true.

"And it's what you want?" her mom asked. "Really?"

Rylee had the distinct feeling that her mother was having a hard time believing this. But what part? She thought she'd been convincing enough. But it was probably just her conscience that was making her paranoid. She hated lying, and it felt like she'd done enough of it to last a lifetime in just the last day alone.

"It's what I want," she said evenly. Ignoring the little angel on her shoulder that was shaking a tiny finger at her.

"Marriage isn't easy, Rylee. Your dad and I have gone through some rough patches that we almost didn't make it through. And then when you have kids, well… You know how hard it's been with your brothers leaving the way they have. How hard on the family that's been. All of those challenges are in front of you, and more. You want to be confident in your partner. Sure that you can weather the storms together. You're *sure* about this?"

Rylee could hear the deeper meaning in her mother's tone. Was she sure that Shep was the one she wanted to weather those storms with? Shep, with his own messed-up family history, and his devil-may-care attitude about life. Rylee felt defensive of him right then, but she could understand her mom's concern. It was natural, even if it wasn't quite fair. Shep had never done anything to hurt her. Still, she guessed it was possible that he could.

"I'm sure, Mom," she said.

"Then if it's what you want, it's what we want for you."

She bit the inside of her cheek. "You mean it?"

"Of course. That doesn't mean we aren't going to worry. We'll worry no matter what. But if you're happy, we're happy."

Rylee smiled, her eyes stinging with surprise tears. She knew this was a leap for her mother, and it meant a lot having her blessing.

And then she remembered this was all just pretend. A very real blessing, for a pretend engagement.

She closed her eyes for a minute and breathed deeply. Saying yet another prayer that everyone would forgive her when the time came.

Chapter Four

Shep glanced over at Rylee in the passenger seat of his truck. It was Friday night, and they hadn't seen each other all week, but had texted for most of it. He'd called her last night and asked if she wanted to go on a date. A pretend date, but still. He'd been looking forward to seeing her for days.

She looked beautiful tonight. They'd settled on a laid-back drink at Doug's in Bronco Valley, but she'd dressed up, and that got him right in the heart. She wore a pretty red dress with a slightly plunging neckline that warmed his blood. Rylee had never been much for makeup, but she had a cherry-red gloss on her lips that made him want to pull the truck over and kiss her long and hard.

He looked back at the road. "Are you ready for this?"

"For what?"

"Our first public outing as an engaged couple."

He glanced over again to see her smile.

"Ready as I'll ever be," she said. "I just hope I'll be convincing enough. It was weird not telling Gabby the truth."

"I know. But I think your reasoning was pretty sound. You'll tell her soon enough."

She nodded, looking out the window into the night. The lights of the farms and ranches were few and far between, and shone like lighthouse beacons through the dark sea of pastures and crops.

"How was it telling your family?" she asked. "You never really said."

At the mention of his family, his shoulders tensed. He'd actually been feeling bad ever since his mom had called him into the kitchen a few days ago, smiling from ear to ear. But he had to admit, it was nice not having to endure the never-ending comments and questions about when he was going to get serious about his personal life, and how much it would mean to his parents to see him happily settled down.

"It was okay," he said. "My brothers were kind of shocked, but happy for me. It felt strange lying to them and my parents. I have to keep reminding myself this is only temporary."

"Right."

"Honestly, though, I never realized just how much my mom has been at me about getting married until now. I knew it was a lot, but it's actually been nearly every day. Every damn day. That's a lot of marriage pressure."

She laughed. "Aww, poor guy. Well, I'm happy to help."

"I'm happy, too. Happy to be taking you out tonight. Have you ever been to Doug's?"

"Nope. I've heard all about it, though. I'm curious about that haunted bar stool."

"Ahh, the bar stool. Just don't sit on it." He winked at her. "Bad luck and tragedy always follows."

"What kind of tragedy?"

"I can think of two marriages breaking up and at least one accident. Best just to steer clear."

Turning his blinker on, he slowed as Doug's finally came

into view. He hadn't been here in a while, but it was always a good time. Lots of tasty nachos, good music, decent drinks. It was where Bronco's locals came to unwind on the weekends, and sometimes it got pretty wild, but tonight, all Shep could think about was the woman beside him. How she smelled, like summer itself, and how she looked—gorgeous in the moonlight streaming in through the truck's windows.

He turned into a parking spot close to the front door, where the music thumped from inside.

Turning the engine off, he looked over at Rylee. "I forgot to ask if you two-step."

She raised her brows. "Two-step?"

"Yeah."

"Oh. No, I don't dance. Janet's birthday party was a rarity, believe me. And that was mostly because of the champagne."

"That's probably because you've had lousy partners. Lucky for you, I'm not lousy."

"Shep…"

He grabbed her hand, just like he used to, and rubbed his thumb over her knuckles. "I'll lead. All you have to do is follow me. If you want to, that is…"

Her eyes were dark in the cab of the truck and reminded him of those pools in the river where the current was slow and gentle, and the water was deep and clear. Rylee had beautiful eyes. A man could get lost in those eyes if he wasn't careful.

"I want to," she said.

And smiled.

Rylee sat in the small booth by the window, waiting while Shep got their drinks. The place was packed. The music was loud, and the clientele was rowdy, to say the least. Not exactly the type of Friday night she was used to, which made it that much better.

Looking around, she leaned her elbows on the table. She could feel the country music reverberating inside her chest, thumping out a rhythm with her heart. She couldn't believe she was here with Shep Dalton. And more than that, they were pretending to be *engaged*.

When he'd helped her out of the truck earlier, a few people were walking by, and he'd pulled her close. He'd leaned down and whispered in her ear, his breath warm against her skin, "Have to make it look believable..."

She shivered now, thinking about it. If making it look believable meant more moments like that, she was fully on board. But she had to be honest, she'd been on board with this crazy idea from the beginning. She didn't think she would've been able to say no if she'd tried. But she hadn't tried. She'd just signed happily on, and despite her worry about lying to her friends and family for a few weeks, she was having so much fun. Then, all of a sudden, the thought of having to say goodbye to this pretend relationship, to Shep in general, made her breathless.

She forced herself to sit up straighter. She'd just have to cross that bridge when she came to it. And if she ended up regretting this ruse, this sexy little adventure, she'd have to chalk it up to life experience in the end. Live and learn, and heal from the broken heart.

Frowning, she gazed out the window to the darkened parking lot beyond. She'd had her heart broken before, of course. She'd been devastated when Tyler had called off their wedding. But that had felt more like a rejection of her than like losing something truly special. She'd loved Tyler, but she'd never been madly *in* love with him. What she had with Shep? It was different. Drastically different, even though it was all smoke and mirrors, and that said a lot.

"Can I buy you a drink?"

She startled and looked up to see a stocky cowboy standing over her. He was handsome, with dark hair curling around the nape of his neck and a slightly cocky tilt to his mouth. She thought he looked familiar. Thanks to the convention center, she worked around cowboys like this all the time—bull riders, calf ropers, team ropers. There were so many. For a single woman with a healthy libido, it wasn't the worst job in the world.

Still, she wasn't used to being asked if she wanted a drink, by a cowboy or anyone else. She just didn't put herself out there enough. Since Tyler, she'd only been on a handful of dates, and they'd all ended with her saying she'd call the next day, but never had. She'd learned it was just easier not to let it get that far. That way she couldn't get hurt. Maybe that was part of the reason why this fake engagement was so tempting. It was like she was getting to live out her fantasies vicariously, without any risk to her heart. At least, that's what it would look like on paper. She knew that her heart was very much at risk, whether this was a fake engagement or not.

She smiled, scanning the room for Shep. "No, thank you. I'm actually—"

And then, suddenly, he appeared. Tall, lean, impossibly good-looking. He patted the other cowboy's back good-naturedly. "Sorry, man. She's with me."

"We're engaged," she said. "To be married." She hadn't needed to add that last part, but she couldn't help it. It was too tempting not to.

"Oh, my apologies," the other man said. He tipped his hat and walked away, disappearing into the rambunctious crowd.

"Geez." Shep set their drinks down and slid into the booth across from her. "I leave you alone for two minutes..."

"That kind of thing doesn't usually happen to me."

"Are you serious?"

"Very."

"I have a hard time believing that."

She smiled. "Why?"

"You have to know why."

Rylee had always thought of herself as a wallflower. She felt like she had a tendency to blend in. The red dress tonight was helping, but she wasn't kidding herself that she was suddenly some kind of man magnet.

Shep leaned forward, his gaze suddenly intense. "Rylee..."

"Hmm?"

"You *do* know why, don't you?"

Her cheeks burned. She was glad it was so dim in the bar, or he might've been able to see her blush.

"I don't actually think you do," he muttered.

The music changed to something slow and sweet. She took another sip of wine, liking how it felt going down. It warmed her throat and belly, and reminded her that she was very much an adult now. Not a girl, no matter how shy she felt sometimes. Those days were long gone.

"Will you dance with me?" Shep asked.

"Now?"

"Well, it's not the two-step, but it'll do." He held out his hand from across the table.

She eyed it. Then, after a second, she put her hand in his and let him help her out of the booth.

It felt like every eye in the bar was on them as Shep led her to the dance floor. Without another word, he pulled her close and wrapped an arm around her waist. His belt buckle bit into her hip, leaving her a little dizzy. It was a strangely sensual feeling.

"I've got you," he whispered, leaning close to her ear. "Just follow my lead."

Whether he was talking about the dancing at this point or their engagement, it didn't really matter. Rylee was completely lost to him right then.

The music thrummed in her ears as she closed her eyes and laid her cheek against his chest. He held her hand tightly in his and splayed the other out on her lower back. His calluses were rough against her palm, his fingers long and blocky and distinctly male. She breathed him in as they moved across the dance floor.

Shep was so confident that she didn't even have to think about where her feet were going next. She found that she loved how that felt. When it came to her career, Rylee had to be dialed in at all times. Since she was in control of so many things at work, she had to be. But when it came to her personal life, she'd forgotten how comforting it was to let someone else show her the way. Even if it was something as small as dancing on a Friday night.

After another minute, the song came to an end, and Shep leaned down and kissed her softly on the cheek. "See?" he said. "You're a natural."

Her face filled with the now familiar heat she felt whenever he did things like this. In front of everyone and with no hesitation at all. Just another thing that she was getting used to. Another thing that she was beginning to love about being in Shep's orbit again after all this time.

"I don't know about that," she said. "You make it easy."

He smiled as they walked off the dance floor and back to their booth.

"It's pretty busy," he said. "I should order our food at the bar, or we might end up waiting forever for a server. Do you know what you want?"

"Oooh, I'd love a cheeseburger," she said. "Everything on it. And fries."

"That's my kind of woman. I'll be right back."

Sliding into the booth again, she watched him cross the crowded room. He was taller than most of the men there and so handsome that she had to catch her breath. How was it that Shep wasn't taken yet? He'd always been wild and a little reckless, someone she had a hard time imagining any woman being able to tame for any length of time. Was that why his mother was so anxious for him to be married? Was she worried about where that wild streak would leave him in the end?

Rylee was still contemplating this when a young woman stepped up to her booth, smiling wide.

"Rylee Parker? I thought that was you!"

Rylee blinked up at her. She looked vaguely familiar, but she couldn't seem to place her. Maybe someone from the convention center? Or from her apartment complex? BH247 was full of twentysomethings, busy with their careers and lives. Sometimes it was hard keeping track of them all.

"I'm sorry, I…"

"Lisa Frye? We went to high school together. I know it seems like a hundred years ago now."

Rylee smiled. Of course. Lisa Frye. She'd been one of Janet's friends. Popular, bubbly, on the cheerleading team.

Not exactly someone Rylee hung out with, but like Janet, she'd always been nice to her.

Lisa looked different now. Gone were the long, blond locks she'd had at seventeen, replaced by a trendy pixie cut and pink-framed glasses. Rylee thought she looked like Tinkerbell, only cuter.

"Can I sit for a minute?" she asked. "My husband is getting us drinks. Might as well catch up."

"Of course! It's so good to see you."

"It's good to see you, too."

"Do you live in Bronco?" Rylee asked, glancing quickly at the bar. Shep was nowhere to be seen. Swallowed up by dozens of people clamoring for drinks.

"No, we're just here visiting my folks," Lisa said, settling into the booth. "They moved a few years ago. William and I are still in Tenacity. I teach third grade there."

"That's great. I bet you're a wonderful teacher."

"You're sweet. I love it, but some days are easier than others." She smiled and dimples appeared in each cheek. "What do you do, Rylee?"

"I work in marketing at the Bronco Convention Center."

"Oh, wow. So, you know Hattie Hawkins, then?"

"Absolutely. I'm a huge fan of Hattie's."

"Me, too. So is my class. We did a lesson last fall about trailblazing women, and Hattie came to talk to them about rodeo. She had them mesmerized. She's quite a lady."

Rylee grinned. Not only was the septuagenarian Hattie a rodeo legend, but she was also a genuinely great person. Her four daughters, known on the circuit as the original Hawkins Sisters, and her granddaughters, members of the newest generation of Hawkins Sisters, were the same. Hattie had raised a family of strong, spirited women, all while working and excelling in a male-dominated field. Rylee couldn't think of anyone more equipped to speak to a class full of starry-eyed kids than Hattie Hawkins.

"She really is," Rylee said.

"So," Lisa said, leaning forward. "Are you married? Kids?"

Rylee cleared her throat, glancing over at the bar again. For some reason, fibbing about being engaged to Shep was much easier when he was sitting right next to her. Fibbing about being engaged when she was sitting by herself felt less like a playful lie and more like a whopping one.

"Well," she began, "I'm actually engaged…"

She hoped that sounded believable. She'd had a hard time getting the words over her vocal cords.

"That's wonderful!" Lisa said. "Who's the lucky man?"

Licking her lips, Rylee tucked her hands in her lap. She didn't have a ring on. What if Lisa asked to see it?

"Shep," she said. "Shep Dalton."

Lisa's hazel eyes widened. "Shep *Dalton*?"

Rylee nodded.

"Shep Dalton from high school? And *you*?"

She nodded again, beginning to feel a prickle of unease. The way Lisa said that made it sound like she couldn't believe Rylee had landed someone like Shep. And that hurt her feelings in a quick rush that took her by surprise.

"I mean," Lisa said quickly, "it's just that I'm shocked he's settling down, that's all. Not that he's settling down with you. You know what I mean."

"He doesn't seem like the settling down type, I know."

"Well, he didn't used to. But I'm sure he's changed. You're going to love being married. Sometimes I wonder how I ever managed before. Not that I *couldn't* manage before, but I'm just so much happier now, you know? It just feels right. Not for everyone, of course, but I bet you'll wonder why you two waited this long."

Rylee took a sip of her wine. Shep was right. The pressure to get married was everywhere. If this was even a hint of what he'd been getting from his mother, she could understand him welcoming this fake engagement with open arms. It made complete sense.

Lisa looked across the room and waved. "Oh, it looks like William has our drinks. It was so great to see you. Tell Shep I said hello, okay?"

"It was good to see you, too," Rylee said. "And I'll tell him. He'll be sorry he missed you."

With a wiggle of her fingers, Lisa slid out of the booth and sauntered away, leaving Rylee with an empty feeling in her stomach. She knew the other woman meant well, but the whole interaction had been unsettling. First, with the way she'd reacted to hearing that Shep was engaged to Rylee (of all people!), and then with the whole marriage thing in general.

Sure, she and Shep would have some fun with this for a while, and it would give him a much-needed breather with his parents, but then what? Rylee had always felt fulfilled without being married, but she'd be lying if she said she hadn't longed for that kind of life deep down. She wanted to be a wife, she wanted to be a mother. Tyler hadn't necessarily wanted a traditional kind of family, dismissing her whenever she brought it up. It had made her sad, and left her feeling like she'd have to fight for it when the time came. It wasn't that she didn't think she could be happy without those things, but she wanted them anyway. The fact that this engagement wasn't real only made her want them even more.

Suddenly, she felt melancholy. Looking out the darkened window, she wondered what was messing with her head so much. Was this about turning thirty? If that was it, at least she was in good company. Her entire graduating class was in the same boat.

Or was it something else? Something deeper and more profound?

She watched a car pulling out of the parking lot, its bright red taillights blazing through the night, and before she could help it, she wondered if this sudden feeling could be because of some*one* and not some*thing*. Someone who'd reappeared in her life after being gone for so long. Someone whom she'd had such feelings for...

Maybe it was Shep himself who had her turned upside down.

Shep made his way back to the booth, weaving in between people who were getting louder and drunker by the minute. He let his gaze settle on Rylee across the room. She had her chin in her hand and was staring out the window. She didn't look like she was having a very good time.

Frowning, he muttered an apology to a woman for jostling her as he passed, but kept his eyes on Rylee. Maybe he shouldn't have brought her here. They'd decided on something low-key for tonight, but she'd gotten all dressed up and everything. She looked so beautiful in that dress. Maybe he should've taken her somewhere nice in Bronco Heights instead. Of course, that would've been like an actual date, instead of just a pretend date, but still. A real date didn't seem like that much of a stretch. They'd kissed, after all. They were engaged, as far as everyone around here knew. Sure, it might be working backward, but what the hell. He was so attracted to her that backward or forward, it didn't really matter to him. Just so long as he got to spend time with her in some form or fashion, he was happy.

But the question was, was she? Shep felt his jaw muscles clench. Would she even have considered going out with him if it weren't for this game they were playing? Asking himself that question wasn't exactly pleasant, since he'd never relished rejection, and Rylee couldn't truly be interested in someone like him long-term. So, *would* she have gone out with him? He didn't really know. All he knew was that he liked what they had going on right now. He liked it a lot. So much so that he didn't want it to end anytime soon. But the problem was, they'd only agreed to a few weeks. Any more than that, and they'd be digging a hole that wouldn't be so easy to dig their way out of. He was trying to keep himself from thinking about his mother, who would be more than disappointed when they fake broke up.

He stepped up to the booth, and Rylee looked up at him with a smile. But he'd been right—she looked different. Not unhappy, necessarily, but definitely bothered by something.

He slid in across from her. "The kitchen is pretty slammed, so our burgers should be ready in about twenty minutes. I hope you're not too starved."

"I think I'll survive that long. Thanks for ordering."

He waited, watching her. Her silky auburn hair fell next to her face in a way that made him want to reach out and touch it. In fact, his fingers itched with it. Dancing with her a few minutes ago had lit something inside him that was now burning ferociously. A need that had doubled since they'd met up at Janet's party. Since spending the night together in that little motel bed.

He shifted uncomfortably and took a deep breath, hoping he didn't look as distracted by her as he felt.

"Do you remember Lisa Frye?" she asked, taking a sip of her wine.

"Lisa Frye...from high school?"

She nodded. "She's here with her husband. You just missed her."

"Ahh. How's she doing?"

"She's a teacher in Tenacity. She asked if I was married, and I told her that you and I were engaged."

He smiled, liking how that sounded. "Oh yeah?"

She didn't smile back. Just kept running her index finger around the rim of her wineglass with her gaze averted.

"Rylee?"

"Hmm?"

"What's wrong?"

She looked up at him, her eyes dark. "Nothing's wrong."

"Now, see. I don't believe that. We used to know each other pretty well, and I recognize that look on your face."

"What look?"

"The one that says something's wrong, but you're trying to hide it."

"You could always read my mind," she said.

"What's going on? Did she say something to upset you?"

She shook her head. "No. I mean...kind of, but I know she didn't mean anything by it."

"What'd she say?"

"She just seemed surprised that we were engaged. Specifically, that you would be engaged to me." She tucked her hair behind her ear. "It's silly. But I guess it brought up some of those old insecurities from when we were kids."

He watched her, leaning back in the booth. It was hard to believe Rylee would feel anything but complete and total confidence, as gorgeous as she was. But she obviously didn't have a clue how he saw her. Or how anyone else saw her, for that matter. Maybe Lisa had been surprised, but it made more sense that she'd be surprised that Rylee would have anything to do with him, not the other way around.

But it was easy to forget how Rylee had been as a girl. The glasses and the shy, quiet way about her. The studiousness and seriousness that had drawn him to her in a way that had been hard to deny, even back then. It was true that he'd wanted to see her let her hair down and have some fun, but he'd loved her personality just as she was. She was different. And different in a town like Tenacity was always a good thing. At least, he'd always thought so.

As she gazed back at him now, though, he could see that she still struggled with those differences. He'd known how hard it had been for her; she'd opened up to him about it more than once. Those insecurities were part of what had driven her to go to college out of state. To push herself out of her comfort zone and to get her MBA and come back to Montana a changed woman. A woman who'd left all that kid stuff behind. But sometimes leaving the kid stuff behind was easier said than done.

He slid out of his seat and came around to her side of the booth.

"Scoot over," he said evenly. "We're engaged. We should be sitting on the same side anyway. It's the law."

She laughed and moved over to give him room.

Sliding in, he put his arm around her. Her body was soft and giving, and he could smell her shampoo. It stirred something inside of him.

"You," he said, "are stunning. I know you don't believe that, you've never believed that, but you are. Don't make me list all the ways."

"Shep…"

"I will, you know."

She shook her head. "Oh God. Don't."

"Why not?"

"It's embarrassing."

"It's embarrassing to hear that you're beautiful?"

She didn't answer that. She just lowered her lashes and licked her lips, reminding him how much he'd been wanting to kiss her again.

"Let's start with those eyes," he said, pretending to stick a dagger in his chest. "I mean, come on. Heartbreaker territory, here."

She laughed.

"No, I'm serious. You're absolutely gorgeous. But that's nothing compared to your smarts, Rylee. Your compassion and warmth. Which, by the way, you have in spades."

"Stop."

"Am I getting through? Making a dent in that armor?"

"You've always been able to get through. You're my Achilles' heel."

"Oooh. I like the sound of that."

She smiled, and he touched her chin with the tips of his fingers, coaxing her to turn her head and look into his eyes.

"Seriously, though," he said, his voice lower this time. "You're the whole package, Rylee."

Her expression softened. Her body relaxed into his, making him wonder how he was ever going to let her go in a few weeks. This wasn't something he wanted to let go of. *She* wasn't something he wanted to let go of. Shep wasn't usually the kind to look too far into the future, but where Rylee was concerned, he couldn't help it. He wanted more.

He swallowed hard, his throat feeling uncomfortably dry. What if he didn't have to let her go? What if this didn't have to end? The thought appeared in his head like a light bulb flashing on, its light warm and bright behind his eyes. *What if...*

Slowly, he took his arm away from her shoulders and reached for his beer. He needed something to wet his tongue. Because the thought that had just occurred to him was beginning to take hold, like a seedling in cool, damp soil. *What if...*

Rylee watched him, her brows furrowed. "What is it?"

Taking a swallow of his beer, he wondered if he should even voice this out loud. It was wild, after all. Wilder than pretending to get engaged, and that was saying something. But if Shep was anything, it was unconventional. He knew that was part of what Rylee liked about him. Or, at least, what she used to like about him. They balanced each other out. She planned things, and he turned them upside down.

"I just had a thought," he said.

"Oh yeah?"

Shifting in the booth, he turned to face her.

"What if we went through with it?" he said.

"Went through with what?"

He waited a beat. Then two. She'd think he'd lost his marbles, but what the hell.

"What if we actually got married?" he asked slowly.

She stared at him. "I'm sorry...what?"

"We made that promise to each other for a reason, right?"

"Shep...we made that promise when we were kids. We had no idea what we were doing."

"We were kids," he said, "but we knew damn well what we were doing. For one thing, we knew each other better than anyone else did. We were best friends."

"Just because we were close—"

"We were best friends."

"Just because we were best friends didn't mean we were serious."

"We were young, but we weren't stupid, Rylee. We knew that marriage could be a practical thing. We also knew that if we got to be a certain age without taking that step with someone else, it just made sense to take it with each other. We already know we're great together. A lot of marriages start out with less than that."

She laughed. "Did you have a couple of shots at the bar or something?"

"I'm stone-cold sober."

"I can't believe you're actually suggesting this."

"Why not? We're not getting any younger. Our families are pumped that we're engaged. Just think how happy they'd be if we actually tied the knot."

"You'd do this just to get them to stop nagging you?"

"No, but that'd be a nice bonus."

She shook her head, but there was a sparkle in her eyes. Maybe she didn't think it was such a nutty idea after all. There was always that possibility.

He nudged her elbow. "No more dead-end dating. We'd always have a built-in plus-one. We'd get to see what's so damn great about being married and still have the safety net of being friends. You're tempted, aren't you?"

"I'm not admitting I'm tempted, but…"

"But?"

"But, there *are* some practical reasons for it."

"See? That's what I'm saying."

"What about all that stuff about you not being the marrying kind?"

He smiled. "That was before."

She touched her temple. "I think I've had too much wine on an empty stomach. I'm actually considering this."

"Look, we don't have to decide anything tonight. But I'm glad you're considering it."

"Wait," she said. "Just wait a minute, Shep…"

He watched her, his gaze dropping to her mouth. If they actually got married, he'd get to look at that mouth every single day. He didn't really care to weigh anything beyond that. At the moment, it was all that mattered.

"Are you *actually* serious about this?" she asked. "I mean, truly?"

He took her hand in his. Before tonight, before he'd seen her in this dress, he would've had to think about that. But that was the thing. He didn't want to think at all. Which a lot of people would say was exactly his problem. Always had been.

Was this just another one of his harebrained ideas that he was going to talk her into? He already knew the answer to that. It was probably selfish, definitely reckless. But he wanted more of her, and she was turning out to be something he was having trouble resisting. And truth be told, he was getting caught up in this engagement thing. It was fun, wild. And those were two things that Shep had *always* had trouble resisting.

"I'm damn serious," he said.

Chapter Five

Rylee stepped out of her car and into the soft spring afternoon. It was unseasonably warm for April in Montana, and she was only wearing jeans and a sweater, but she shivered anyway, looking over at the sprawling ranch house and the big, fancy barn and riding facility beyond that.

It was her first time at Dalton's Grange, and it was just as beautiful as she'd imagined. Neal and Deborah had bought a gorgeous property with wide-open pastures for their cattle and views of the jagged, snowcapped mountains in the distance.

She took a deep breath, the air smelling sweet, like horses and grass, and tried to ignore the nerves in her belly. Shep had assured her this was just a casual visit. Maybe they'd go on a horseback ride or a picnic or something, but most of his family was in Helena for the weekend for a stock show, so the pressure was off. He'd wanted it to be a laid-back introduction to his ranch, but she was anxious anyway because she knew Deborah had stayed behind, and she was the one person Rylee was most nervous about seeing again.

Her phone dinged from her pocket, and she pulled it out to see a text from Shep.

When you get here, just go on up to the house. I have to check on one of our pregnant cows really quick. Won't be long. Just make yourself at home!

She bit the inside of her cheek, tucking the phone back in her pocket. He'd told her earlier that his mom was in town for the morning, so the house was empty. Still, she'd be back at some point, and then what? All of a sudden, the nerves in her belly multiplied at the thought of making small talk with the woman who thought Rylee was going to be her new daughter-in-law. Poor Deborah. She had no idea she was being deceived. Unless, of course, Shep and Rylee got married after all.

At the thought of Shep's suggestion the other night, Rylee grazed her teeth over her bottom lip. She still couldn't believe that he'd been serious, but he was. Dead serious. She still couldn't get her mind around the idea of marrying Shep. She'd left Doug's the other night without giving him an answer, but ever since he'd dropped her off afterward, she'd been thinking about it. She couldn't *stop* thinking about it. There were two ways to look at this outrageous proposal. One, they'd be digging themselves in even deeper by actually getting married. Something that would require more than a fake breakup to fix. They'd actually have to get an annulment or, worse, a divorce if it didn't work out. And what were the odds that it would work out? Shep hadn't said one word about being in love with her. He'd only mentioned the convenience of it. Because that was what a union between them would be, after all. A marriage of convenience.

Rylee hitched her purse up over her shoulder and began walking slowly toward the house. The *other* way of thinking about it was the most tempting option. They wouldn't have to have a fake breakup. They wouldn't have to disappoint anyone or admit that they'd rushed into an engagement without thinking it all the way through, which was, of course, what everyone would assume. But the absolute best part would be that she'd be getting married to Shep. No matter what he thought about it, it would be a secret dream come true for her. Getting to marry her high-school crush. She could hardly imagine it without wanting to squeal like a girl. Which was ridiculous, but that was how she felt.

However, she also felt a fair amount of hesitation, which was her brain taking over from her heart. Shep didn't love her. That much was obvious. And did she want to get married to someone who didn't love her, even if it *was* a marriage of convenience? She didn't think of herself as being overly traditional, but she was traditional enough to believe that love and marriage still went hand in hand. Tyler had never loved her, not really. A realization that still hurt to this day. It was something that always made her feel small whenever she revisited the memories of that relationship.

She took the stairs up to the lovely wraparound front porch, where two rocking chairs sat facing the north pasture, just waiting for someone to come sit and rest and contemplate. Hanging baskets full of colorful spring pansies lined the overhang, smelling heavy and sweet. Horses nickered in the distance, and Rylee could imagine living here, sitting on the porch and drinking lemonade on hot summer afternoons or cooking dinner in the kitchen and hearing the thudding of cowboy boots coming down the hallway. It was a big, fancy ranch, but it was also a home where family gathered and lived and loved. Her own modest home in Tenacity felt empty these days, with her brothers gone and her parents rattling around in it alone.

She came to a stop at the front door, where a bronze flower wreath hung, and felt an ache inside her heart that took her by surprise. As much as she loved her apartment in BH247, she missed being around family like this. She missed a wood fire in the hearth on winter nights and home-cooked meals and having someone to share them with. Even a marriage of convenience would still be a marriage. She'd be welcomed into this life; she'd settle into this family. And before she could help herself, she imagined what it would be like to walk through this front door on Shep's arm, as his wife, as his partner.

It was a thought that warmed her through, even as she raised her hand to knock on the door like a stranger would. Shep had said to go on inside, but that felt assuming to her, so she waited a few seconds and knocked again, just to make sure nobody was inside.

When she was positive she wasn't going to be surprising anyone, especially Deborah, she turned the handle and pushed the door open.

Standing in the doorway for a minute, she looked around with her heart in her throat. The house was absolutely stunning. With its rustic leather couches and chairs, and darkly stained wood, it looked like something out of a home decor show. There was a giant antler chandelier hanging from the ceiling, something that would have been too much in any other space but fit perfectly here. She wondered if Deborah had decorated the house herself or had brought in someone to do it for her. Regardless, it was beautiful, and Rylee had to catch her breath at the sight.

From across the house, a door slammed.

"Hello?" she called hesitantly, painfully aware that she was standing in his parents' living room after having just let herself in.

"Shep, honey? Is that you?"

Her stomach twisted. *Deborah.* She must've been out back when Rylee pulled up. Not only was she going to have to explain why she'd walked right in, but she was also going to have to talk about the engagement, which she'd been wanting to avoid for as long as possible. Lying to Gabby was bad enough, but lying to Shep's mother was going to be especially hard to do. Second only to lying to her own mother.

"Um…" She steeled herself. "Actually, it's me, Mrs. Dalton. Rylee Parker. Remember?"

Deborah appeared in the kitchen doorway, looking fit and polished. She wore a pair of dark-wash jeans with a turquoise belt and a pink plaid Western shirt that complimented her dewy skin tone. She looked exactly the same as Rylee remembered.

"Rylee!" she said, slapping her thigh. "What are you doing here?"

Rylee felt herself blush all the way to her ears. "Shep invited me. He's out with the cows. I'm so sorry to surprise you. I knocked, but there was no answer."

"Are you kidding?" She stepped forward and pulled Rylee into a perfumed hug. "You're family!"

Stepping back again, Deborah grinned. "I've been wanting him to ask you over for a proper supper, but he didn't want us bombarding you. I'm just so happy to see you. It's been years! And now this." She shook her head. "Well, I just can't believe it."

Rylee felt her stomach drop like a stone. All of a sudden, the guilt was overwhelming. "I know it must've been a shock, Mrs. Dalton…"

"Deborah, please! It was, but in the best way possible. Come sit down. I'll make a pot of tea. Do you like tea? I can't remember."

Rylee let herself be ushered over to the couch, where she sat, feeling about an inch tall. Deborah was so sweet, so warm and welcoming, and she had no clue that this engagement wasn't real. The whole thing had seemed pretty harmless in the beginning. Fun and carefree, like Shep himself. But now it was obvious that people could be hurt by this. Definitely disappointed.

Deborah sat across from her on the love seat.

"I can't get anything out of Shepard," she said. "Tell me everything. And show me that ring!"

"Oh…uh…" Rylee clasped her hands in her lap. She really needed to fish something out of her jewelry box at home. What kind of newly engaged woman went around without her ring?

"Mom?"

They both turned to see Shep standing there, hat in hand, a ring around his dark blond hair. His face looked flushed. Like he might've run to get here.

"What are you doing here?" he asked. Probably knowing very well that he'd just interrupted an engagement interrogation.

Deborah laughed. "Well, I live here, honey."

"I mean, what are you doing back from town so early?"

"I didn't get groceries… What does it matter? And why didn't you tell me you were inviting my soon-to-be daughter-in-law over?"

Rylee watched him as he walked over then leaned down to give her a kiss on the lips. It was so natural, so believable, she almost forgot it was all for show.

"Hey, baby," he said, then sat down next to her and took her hand. "Sorry, Mom. I just didn't want Rylee feeling overwhelmed or anything."

"Am I that bad?"

"Of course not… It's just that—"

"I'm a little shy," Rylee interjected, trying to help. "But you're absolutely right, I should've come before this."

"Well, you're here now!" Deborah leaned forward, trying to get a look at Rylee's hand.

Shep cleared his throat. "If you're looking for the ring, I haven't gotten one yet."

Deborah stared at him, incredulous. "What do you mean you haven't gotten one yet?"

"I proposed on the spur of the moment. It wasn't planned."

"Still, son. It's been over a week. You need to get this girl a ring."

Rylee resisted the urge to squirm. She felt like she was sitting outside her own body, watching all of this happen to someone else.

"You know," Deborah said, looking thoughtful, "I've got Grandma's engagement ring. It's just gathering dust. It's old-fashioned, so you'd probably want to reset the diamond, but you kids are welcome to it. I know she'd be so pleased about that."

Rylee felt her eyes widen. "Oh… I don't…"

"Mom," Shep said, "that's really sweet. But we'll need to talk about it. You know."

"Of course, of course. But it's here if you want it."

Shep turned to Rylee, looking like he'd bitten off more

than he could chew. They'd *both* bitten off more than they could chew. "Want to saddle up the horses?" he asked. "Go for a ride?"

He probably knew how anxious she was to make her escape. The nicer Deborah was, the more she wanted to run away.

"That sounds great."

Deborah smiled. "Okay. Well, you kids have fun. But we're going to have dinner soon, okay? No excuses. With the whole family."

Shep nodded. "The whole family. Got it."

Still holding on to Rylee's hand, he stood up. She stood, too, and leaned into his side. She hoped she looked appropriate. Like a young woman engaged and in love. Instead of how she felt, which was like a huge liar.

After giving Deborah a hug goodbye, she followed Shep out the door and onto the porch. The April sunshine was warm on her cheeks, and the breeze felt good after the sudden claustrophobic feeling of the house.

"Oh my God," Shep breathed. "I'm sorry about that. She wasn't even supposed to be here."

"I feel terrible," Rylee said, following him down the steps.

"It'll be okay. She's excited, but she'd be all right if we broke up. She'd make it."

"If we fake broke up. Since we're not really engaged to begin with."

"Well. Yeah. But you're forgetting, we could go through with it, you know."

"You're nuts."

"Maybe. But you love it."

She smiled, unable to help it.

"Should I list all those practical reasons again?" he continued, walking close to her. She was acutely aware of how his arm felt brushing up against hers. How she'd prefer it around her waist, his thumb moving back and forth on her hip, leaving her skin tingling in its wake.

"I'm aware of all the practical reasons."

"Good. Saves me the trouble."

"I still can't believe you're serious about this," she said.

"You saw my mom in there. You can clearly see what I'm up against. What I've been dealing with this whole time."

"Still, that's not a reason to get *married*, Shep."

"No, that alone isn't a reason. But there are other reasons. Good reasons. You know it as well as I do."

"It's not exactly how I've pictured this marriage thing my whole life."

"Traditional?" He shook his head, putting his Stetson back on. He pulled it low over his eyes, so he looked sexy and brooding. "No. But what's so great about traditional, anyway? Traditional is boring. And we, Rylee Parker, are not boring."

"Maybe you aren't. But I'm fairly predictable."

"Now, that's where you're wrong. A predictable woman would not have entered into a fake engagement. Nor would she be considering getting married to her fake fiancé. Just saying."

"No, I guess not."

"See?"

"I feel awful about your mother."

"I know. I do, too. But it'll work out. She might not ever have to know we've been fibbing."

"Fibbing is a nice way to put it. We've been lying." She rubbed her temple. "Gabby is going to kill me."

"She won't kill you."

"She will. She'll murder me in my sleep. And I can't blame her. I'd be so mad if I found out she kept something like this from me."

He came to a stop and touched her arm, until she stopped, too. Then took her shoulders in his hands and gently turned her so she was facing him.

"Then let's make sure they don't find out."

She looked up at him. Wanting more than anything to follow his lead, but afraid to at the same time.

"I don't know about you," he said softly, "but I could do without all the damn stuff leading up to marriage. I've been there. I've dated, and *that* bores me. This is anything but boring."

Chewing the inside of her cheek, she let that settle. She thought about Lisa the other night and how clearly surprised she'd been when she heard about this engagement. That had hurt. But could Rylee blame her? She'd always felt the same way. Like Shep would never really be interested in someone like her. And even if their marriage was for convenience only, how long would it be until he got tired of it? Until he got tired of her? The need to protect herself from that eventual pain was overwhelming as he stood there looking down at her. So handsome that her heart literally ached from it.

"I think we might be in over our heads here," she said, forcing herself to look away. "I am, anyway."

Reaching up, he ran the back of his knuckles along her cheekbone. His skin was rough, but his touch was unbelievably gentle. It sent chills all the way to her scalp.

"Do you trust me, Rylee?" he asked.

"It's not about trusting you. We're not kids anymore, Shep."

"No, we're not. And that's exactly why I want to do this."

"Getting married just because it's convenient isn't the right reason to get married."

"Then what *is* the right reason?"

"Oh, I don't know. That you're in love, maybe? That you want to spend the rest of your life with someone?"

"I do love you," he said. "I've always loved you. Best friends, remember?"

It was hard to argue with that. Still, he had to know what she really meant. He was just skirting the issue because this was something he wanted, and that was what Shep did.

"And you're wrong when you say that getting married because it's convenient isn't a good reason to get married," he continued. "But I wouldn't use the word *convenient*, I'd use the word *easy*. Things between us have always been easy, and that's a fantastic reason to get married. I've seen people get married because they fall in love or lust or whatever. And then they've got nothing left when that feeling fades. We already have a rock-solid foundation. We could build on that. If it doesn't work, it doesn't work, but at least we could say we tried. And that we kept our promise to each other. Which I was serious about, by the way. Doesn't matter that I was a kid. I knew what I wanted then, and I know what I want now."

She ran her tongue over her lips, and his gaze dropped to her mouth. Her belly immediately tightened at the expression on his face.

"And I'm what you want now?" she asked.

He didn't answer. Instead, he leaned toward her. So close that she could feel his breath against her face. She could see the flecks of hazel in his eyes. It reminded her of the river rock near their swimming hole all those years ago. Honey brown and catching the sun like molten gold.

And then, he kissed her. Her heart was beating so hard, so fast, that she could feel its cadence in her ears. Her pulse skipped in her wrists as he wrapped an arm around her and pulled her close. His tongue flicked against her lips, lightly but insistently, until she opened her mouth and invited him in.

Rylee didn't think she'd ever been kissed like this before. So deeply that she saw stars exploding in colorful bursts behind her eyes, like firecrackers on the Fourth of July. She'd asked him if he wanted her, and it turned out that he didn't have to answer at all. Not with words, at least.

She could feel it in his kiss.

"I cannot believe I had to hear this from Brady Sellers down at the damn feed store," Morgan said, his baseball cap pulled low over his eyes.

Shep tucked his gloved hands underneath the twine of another hay bale and hauled it off the truck. Sweat dripped into his eyes, making them sting with a viciousness that made him blink over at his brother now. Morgan looked pissed. And Morgan pissed was not a fun guy to be around. At least, not for any length of time.

"I know," he said, heaving the hay bale toward the barn. It tumbled a few times before coming to a rest near his brother's boots. "Honestly, we weren't expecting it to get around so fast. It just…did."

"Could you please not chuck these things at me?" Morgan said, leaning over to straighten the bale out so it aligned with the rest of them. "There's a way to do this, you know."

"Yeah, I know. The fast way."

Shep grabbed another bale and hauled it over the side of the truck. But this time, he walked over a few steps to set it down neatly next to the others.

"See?" Morgan said. "That wasn't so hard."

Shep rolled his eyes and rubbed the back of his glove underneath his sweaty chin.

"Now, tell me why I had to hear about my little brother being engaged from Brady," Morgan said. "And don't give me the crap you gave Mom about not wanting to overwhelm Rylee."

"I'm sorry." Shep leaned against the side of the Ford for a breath and took his Stetson off. The breeze felt good in his hair. He'd hung his jacket on the fence post a while ago, and he could feel the warmth of the late afternoon sun start to burn the back of his neck. "But you remember how shy Rylee is. And our family? Come on."

"She comes from a big family, too. Lots of brothers, as I recall. She knows how it works."

"All the more reason to keep it on the down-low for a while. But I'm sorry I didn't tell you guys. I was going to."

"Uh-huh."

"I was."

"Right."

"Are you gonna pout now?"

"Shut up."

Shep smiled at his big brother. Giving him a hard time was one of his favorite pastimes. But Morgan was absolutely right. He should've said something. Now all his brothers were pissed at him to varying degrees because they all thought it was their duty to give him marriage advice before he actually got married. The fact that he was already engaged without their nuggets of wisdom strategically planted in Shep's brain irked them to no end.

"This is not something to enter into lightly," Morgan said, crossing his arms over his broad chest.

Shep had to work not to groan. Now that Morgan was married, he thought of himself as an expert on the subject. It was true that he and Erica had a great relationship, and he was helping to raise Josie, her daughter. But Shep could remember a time when Morgan had been just as much of a train wreck when it came to commitment as Shep was. It was hard to listen to his lectures and not want to throw that back in his face a little.

"I know, Morgan," he said.

"You obviously don't know if you just popped the question on the spur of the moment, for God's sake."

Shep bit his tongue. He had a point there.

"Now, Rylee's great—we all love her—but are you absolutely sure this is what you want?" Morgan looked at him hard. Unrelenting. It was the kind of look a father would give his son. Shep's brothers had always been better role models than his own dad.

"I know it's fast," Shep said. "I'm not arguing that. But this is Rylee we're talking about here."

"Yeah, I know. But is it what you want, Shep? Really?"

Shep scraped a hand through his hair. If he was being honest with himself, he'd say that he hadn't stopped to ask that question since he'd kissed Rylee at Janet's party. Sure, he wanted to sleep with her. And he didn't want any of this to end yet, and getting married seemed like the natural thing to do. Everything he'd told Rylee the other day had been true—they were good together. All the other stuff would work itself out.

But now, with Morgan staring a hole right through him, he had to take a breath and slow down, at least a little, and think about what this really meant.

Marriage... It was a serious commitment, regardless of how he'd been treating it. If it didn't work out, it would mean embarrassment for Rylee. He didn't really give a crap what people around Bronco thought of him, but he cared what they said about Rylee. And he cared that she'd be hurt by it.

He looked out over the north pasture where all the cattle were grazing in the sun. The truth was, knowing all that, he probably shouldn't have pushed this whole marriage thing. But he had. Because at the moment, he *did* think it would work out. There was nothing to complicate it, like most relationships had from the get-go. Rylee wasn't in love with him, something that most likely bothered her, but the way he figured, it only made things easier.

He looked back at Morgan, who was watching him with those eagle eyes. Ready with another epic lecture, no doubt. But Shep wasn't interested. He knew what he wanted, and he wanted Rylee. If that made him a selfish bastard, so be it.

"It's what I want," he said evenly.

Morgan seemed to contemplate this. Then he nodded slowly. "Okay, then. But you need to bring her out for supper, Shep. Let Mom fawn over her a little. Do it right. Rylee deserves that. And honestly, Mom does, too."

Shep tried to ignore a sharp pang of guilt as those words settled. She did deserve that. The only thing was,

Morgan had no idea that she and Shep had been leading everyone astray from the beginning. At the thought of his family finding out now, there was an uncomfortable tightening in his gut.

"Soon," Morgan said. "Okay? No excuses."

Shep nodded and put his Stetson back on, hoping his brother couldn't read the look on his face. The one that might betray every damn thought he was having.

Chapter Six

Rylee walked alongside Gabby in downtown Bronco Heights, the afternoon sun warm on her shoulders. She winced stepping off the curb when the light changed. She couldn't believe how sore she was from riding the other day. There was a time when she'd been more comfortable on horseback than on her own two feet, but those days were long gone. As evidenced by her screaming hamstrings.

Gabby looked over and smiled. They'd just had lunch and were now window-shopping, one of their favorite things to do on Saturday afternoons. But today felt different. Maybe because there was a fairly significant secret between them, something that Rylee hated.

"I told Ryan we'd be a little longer today," Gabby said. "So he's taking Bella to the park."

"Why are we going to be longer?" But Rylee already knew the answer to that. Gabby had been trying to get her to come downtown for days so they could stop in at Beaumont and Rossi's Fine Jewels to look at engagement rings. And down the street from that was Ever After, *the* bridal boutique in town. Rylee had only ever heard about it before. Shopping there was supposed to be quite the experience. Complete with champagne and pastel macarons up the wazoo.

She shoved her hands in her pockets, more aware than ever that she was ringless. Something everyone probably thought was beyond strange, considering she and Shep were supposed to have been engaged for a few weeks now. Rylee never realized how much people wanted to see your ring when you got engaged. It was the first thing they did when they found out—they grabbed your hand to take a look. Then asked when the big day was.

"Come on," Gabby said. "I know you're not big on jewelry, but this is your engagement ring! We can just take a quick peek inside and see if anything catches your eye. *Please*, Ry?"

"Well…"

Gabby hooked her arm in Rylee's as they passed people on the sidewalk clutching their shopping bags and iced coffees. It was such a nice afternoon, and Gabby was so excited for her. Rylee was caught somewhere between feeling excited herself and feeling like crap for lying to her best friend.

She thought about kissing Shep the other day at Dalton's Grange. And how right that had felt, how perfect. Was it crazy to think something might actually work between them? That they could let this fake engagement carry them away to someplace very real and just as magical?

"Well, what?" Gabby said, looking over at her with an exaggerated pout on her pretty face.

Rylee smiled, unable to help it. "Okay," she said. "Let's do it."

"*Yes!* I didn't want to push, but of course I'm going to push. I mean, I have to be involved in helping you pick it out, right? That seems reasonable to me."

"Very reasonable."

"Can I ask you a question, though? Bestie to bestie?"

"Sure."

The smile faded on Gabby's lips as they continued down the sidewalk, their boots tapping out a steady cadence on the cement.

"Why have you been dragging your feet on the ring, Rylee? Tell me honestly. Is it because you're having doubts about this engagement?"

Rylee's stomach dropped. Gabby knew her so well, of course this question was inevitable. In fact, she was surprised her friend hadn't asked before today. Wasn't going to look at rings probably the very first thing she and Shep should've done together?

"It's so fast," she said. "I'm just nervous."

"I get it. I'd feel the same way. But you love him, right? You love Shep?"

"I've always loved him." That was true. But was she *in* love with him? It was a good question because they were two very different things.

"So, you're just nervous," Gabby said. "Nothing else is going on?"

Rylee shook her head. She couldn't bring herself to deny it out loud.

"Good. Then we can look at rings, and maybe a dress or two before we go home."

"You didn't say anything about dresses."

"No, because I knew you'd probably try to run away, if your body language is any indication."

"I'm not *that* bad."

"Girl, you're stiff as a board."

"I've been the one helping you out of your shell since we met," Rylee said. "When did the tables turn, anyway?"

"Getting engaged to Ryan has taught me a lot. I'm much better at getting what I want now. And what I want is for you to try on these rings."

They slowed as the sign for Beaumont and Rossi's came into view. Rylee's heart skipped in her chest.

"Here we are," Gabby said. "Ready?"

"Ready."

Gabby reached out and pulled the door open. A little bell tinkled their arrival as Rylee stepped inside and looked around. Sparkling glass cases lined the walls, and a crystal chandelier hung low, bathing the entire place in soft light. Expensive-looking paintings hung throughout, and small sculptures accentuated the jewelry cases. They were for sale. Rylee leaned forward and looked at the small price tag on one of them. She almost coughed in astonishment.

"May I help you ladies?"

A tall, graceful woman in an impeccable cream pantsuit appeared from behind the front counter. She wore her hair in a low French twist and looked like someone out of Rylee's mom's favorite rom-com, *Pretty Woman*. Hopefully she wouldn't be as rude as the sales ladies were in that infamous shopping scene.

"Yes," Gabby said. "My best friend is getting married, but she hasn't picked out a ring yet."

The woman smiled wide. "Well, you're in the right place, I assure you. What kind of ring are you looking for?"

Rylee's cheeks warmed. She thought of how sweet Deborah had been the other day, offering her mother's ring. Honestly, that was more in line with what she'd pick for herself. She'd always been a sucker for sentimental things, and she couldn't think of anything more meaningful than a family heirloom like that.

But she leaned forward anyway and peered inside the cases. She didn't think she'd ever seen such beautiful rings in her life. Every size and shape and color imaginable. They twinkled underneath the chandelier lighting, the diamonds and other precious stones drawing her in as if they were magnetized.

"Oh my gosh," Gabby breathed. "Look at that one."

Her friend pointed to a simple oval-cut solitaire that was big enough to choke a horse.

"That's a lovely choice," the saleslady said, leaning down to unlock the case. "And it would look so nice on you with your delicate hands."

Rylee smiled, resisting the urge to look down at her hands. Did she have delicate hands? She'd never thought about it before.

The saleslady brought out the ring, which was even more stunning up close. It was also bigger up close.

"Here," she said. "Why don't you try it on for size?"

Rylee held out her hand, and the saleslady slipped it on. The cold weight of the stone gave her butterflies. Was she *really* thinking about marrying Shep Dalton?

She stood there staring down at the ring, moving her hand back and forth to make it sparkle.

"That. Is. *Gorgeous*," Gabby said. "It looks so pretty on you, Ry."

"It really does," the saleslady agreed. "A truly classic cut, something that's simple, yet refined."

Rylee took a deep, steadying breath. And then, all of a sudden, she was imagining Shep slipping a wedding band atop this ring at the altar. She pictured her dress, which would also be simple, yet refined. Lace, maybe. Or silk. She imagined her friends and family smiling up at her from the church pews, everyone basking in the bride and groom's obvious happiness on their wedding day.

It was such a sweet thought that she startled when Gabby nudged her shoulder.

"Are you okay?" her friend asked. "You drifted off for a second there."

"Oh…" Rylee smiled, embarrassed. "Fine. I was just thinking."

"About?"

"You asked before if I'd been having doubts. Honestly, sometimes I do wonder if I'm ready for this."

She'd recently gotten her promotion at the convention center. She had her own apartment, her own life, and she called the shots. She liked it that way. But now, standing here with this beautiful ring on her finger—which symbolized so much more than just marriage; it symbolized a whole different *life*—she knew she'd been fooling herself for a while now. Maybe she wanted to be a wife and mother more than she even realized.

"I'm just surprised at how much I want it," she continued softly. "That's all. It scares me, whether I'm ready for it or not."

Gabby put an arm around her shoulder. "Of course you want it, Rylee. When are you going to start trusting the good things that happen to you? Not every guy is going to turn out like Tyler. Not everyone is going to break your heart."

She managed a smile. But *scared* really wasn't a strong enough word.

She was terrified.

* * *

Rylee stood at the window in the convention center's nicest conference room, the one that was reserved for the most important meetings with the most important people, and looked down into the spacious indoor arena. Tori Hawkins was running barrels with a gorgeous sorrel gelding that Rylee knew was as green as the day was long. But you'd never know it. Tori, one of rodeo pioneer Hattie Hawkins's granddaughters, had the horse dialed in, tearing around the barrels like a bat out of hell, but never clipping a single one. If Rylee had to guess, she'd say this was another championship duo in the making.

Looking at her watch, she frowned. She had a meeting with Celeste Montgomery this morning, who'd be here any minute. Celeste was a sports reporter for an ABC Chicago affiliate, and she had just arrived in Bronco last month to cover the rodeo beat. Rylee had met her a few times and liked her a lot. But it was clear that she didn't know anything about rodeo. She was a tough cookie though, and Rylee had no doubt that she'd make this assignment work. Besides, in Rylee's experience, most people fell in love with this sport after they'd been properly introduced to it. That wasn't to say that Celeste would, but the odds were definitely in her favor.

"Oh my God, I stopped for a coffee and got caught in Bronco's morning rush hour. Who knew?"

Rylee turned to see Celeste walk through the door wearing a chic blue pantsuit, with a matching jacket and leather tote hooked over her arm. She was still wearing her sunglasses, and her straight black hair was obviously just blown out. She clutched a coffee in one hand and her phone in the other and looked every bit the big-city reporter.

"You're right on time," Rylee said with a smile. "It's so nice to see you again."

"You too, Rylee."

Celeste took off her sunglasses, putting them on top of her head. She had big, dark eyes and a flawless, khaki-brown complexion. She was absolutely beautiful. Rylee glanced down at her own pantsuit, gray and a little drab in comparison. She just wasn't used to calling attention to herself in any form or fashion. But she remembered how it felt when Shep had first seen her in her red dress the night they'd gone to Doug's. His mouth had literally hung open, and he'd stared at her for a good five seconds, making Rylee's face heat in the best way possible. Maybe she should start dressing like that more often. Maybe it was time to start letting her hair down a little. Even if it was just in the wardrobe department. For some reason, knowing that she was involved with a man like Shep gave her courage where she'd lacked it before. That felt good. Actually, it felt great.

"I should've picked up a coffee for you," Celeste said, stepping up to the window and looking down into the arena. "I don't know what I was thinking."

"That's okay. I've had my fair share of caffeine this morning. Any more and I'd probably be able to fly out of here."

Celeste laughed, but kept her gaze on the horse and rider below. "Who's that?"

"Tori Hawkins."

"Ahh. Of the famous Hawkins Sisters?"

"Indeed."

"I can't believe how fast they take those barrels and manage to stay on. I mean, if that was me…"

"Oh, I know, right? I'd fall off right out of the gate."

Celeste turned to Rylee and took a sip of her coffee. Then set it down on the glossy conference-room table with a sigh. "Between you and me, I'm clueless about barrel racing. And bull riding. And calf roping, and…all of it, really. Chicago isn't exactly the rodeo capital of the world. But they wanted someone who wasn't afraid of a challenge, and I guess that was me."

"Well, you'll learn fast. There's still a lot that I'm figuring out, too, but the people around here are friendly and helpful. If you have a question, they'll do their best to give you an answer. And if they don't know, they'll find you someone who does."

"That's good to know."

"How are you settling into Bronco? Are you liking it so far?"

Celeste ran a hand through her hair. "It's different. A lot of cowboys, that's for sure."

"Not a fan of cowboys?"

"Now, I didn't say that." Celeste gave her a knowing smile. "I can appreciate a handsome man when I see one. But the culture is different. It takes some getting used to."

Rylee knew that was true. She'd gone from Montana to California, and that had been a huge shock to her system. She couldn't imagine what it would be like coming from a city like Chicago to a town like Bronco.

"How about you?" Celeste asked. "I know you're not from here originally, isn't that right?"

Rylee shook her head. "No, I'm from Tenacity. A little town not far from here."

"And you're liking Bronco?"

"I like it. It's faster moving than Tenacity, that's for sure."

"I heard someone say you're recently engaged," Celeste said. "Congratulations."

"Oh…thank you."

Rylee sat down next to Celeste in one of the cushy chairs. The leather was cold, and she shivered. She still couldn't get used to how fast this engagement news had traveled. And was still traveling.

"Are you getting married in Bronco?" Celeste asked. "Or are you going back to Tenacity for that?"

Rylee chewed her bottom lip. It was obvious the other woman was a natural reporter. Her questions were direct, her mannerisms a mixture of relaxed and confident.

"I haven't really thought about it yet," she said.

"I'm sure there's a lot to consider, with family and everything."

Rylee guessed there would be. She wondered how her mother would feel about her getting married in Bronco. Or how Deborah would feel about Shep getting married in Tenacity. The latter made more sense because the Daltons were from there originally.

She cleared her throat. The other day, she'd let herself start imagining her wedding dress. Now she was mentally deciding on the location. If only Celeste knew this was a fake engagement. What in the world would she think?

The other woman leaned back in her chair and took another sip of coffee. "So…" she said, putting her cup down again. "Speaking of cowboys, my boss wants an exclusive from Geoff Burris. That's why I'm here. But he's apparently such a superstar that his people keep putting me off."

"Oh. Well, I'm sure it's nothing personal. He's actually in Europe with his fiancée right now."

"I heard that. But I've asked to Skype, or whatever is easiest for him, and still nothing. It's super frustrating."

Rylee frowned. As the Bronco Convention Center's new marketing director, this was exactly the type of thing she needed to make happen for Celeste. Difficult, though, since she knew Geoff was probably tired of giving interviews. It was why he was in Europe in the first place. Celeste was right when she said he was a superstar. Around here, he was *the* superstar.

"I'm so sorry," Rylee said, leaning forward and spreading her hands out on the cold marble tabletop. "Don't worry, though. This is going to work out. If we can't get Geoff to sit down with you, how about one of his brothers? I can assure you they're very knowledgeable, very successful in rodeo, too."

Celeste tapped her index finger against her coffee cup. "Hmm. Normally, I'd be a stickler for Geoff, but I really need this interview sooner rather than later."

"Let me make a call. Set something up for you."

Celeste gazed past Rylee's shoulder and out the window, obviously weighing this. Then nodded slowly. "Okay," she said. "Thanks, Rylee. I appreciate that."

"Of course. I know you won't be disappointed. The Burris family is wonderful."

"All I know is how they've paved the way for Black rodeo riders in this country, and that's a good story. And I'm all about a good story."

Rylee had no doubt Celeste was about the *best* stories, if the determined look on her face was any indication. She wondered which brother might be the best choice for the interview—Mike, who was engaged to Corinne Hawkins, Jack, or Ross. Ross (a popular bachelor) was also a well-known charmer, which might be perfect for this kind of thing. Of course, Celeste would probably be able to see through all that, but still, a little charm might go a long way. She picked up her phone and added a reminder to call him as soon as this meeting was over. The sooner, the better.

Before she could set her phone back down, it dinged with a text from Shep.

Dinner with the family this weekend? Have you decided whether you're going to marry me or not? Don't break my heart ;)

She must've made a sound, because Celeste looked over curiously.

"It's just my fiancé," she said, managing a smile. "Asking about dinner plans for the weekend…"

Well. Kind of. Not a romantic dinner. Dinner with his entire family. All his brothers and their significant others. But most importantly, Neal and Deborah. If she thought the other day at Dalton's Grange was nerve-racking, just wait until she sat down to an actual meal with all of them.

"That sounds nice," Celeste said. "What's your fiancé's name?"

"Shep. Dalton. Shep Dalton."

Celeste smiled. "You seem nervous."

"I do?"

"You do. Are you okay?"

"Fine. Super."

"Is it pre-wedding jitters? I've heard that's a thing."

If she had pre-wedding jitters, that would mean she was actually getting *married*. Was she getting married? All of a sudden, her head was spinning.

Celeste leaned forward and put a hand on her arm. "Seriously, Rylee. Are you sure you're all right? You're white as a sheet."

"I am?"

"Here. Let me get you some water."

The other woman stood, walked over to the water cooler in the corner of the room and filled a paper cup.

"If you've been busy planning the wedding," Celeste said, bringing it back to Rylee, "you could be overly stressed. Even dehydrated. If it weren't for my coffee, I think I'd forget to drink anything at all. You know how it is when you get busy with work."

Rylee took a sip of the water, which felt heavenly going down. "Thank you. Maybe I am a little stressed."

Celeste sat down again, watching her closely. "That's better. I think the color is coming back."

"Sorry. That's never happened to me before."

"Don't be sorry. Just drink all that water and take a few deeps breaths. That always helps me when I'm feeling panicky."

Rylee breathed in through her nose and out through her mouth. Once, twice, until she felt her pulse begin to slow. Where was this coming from? Was she just nervous about sitting down with Shep's family? That was understandable, but she thought it was more than that. She was pretty sure it had more to do with how she felt about Shep, without him feeling the same way about her. It had been bothering her for a few days now, but she'd pushed it aside in favor of letting herself get swept up in all of this. It was easy to do.

She took another sip of water and smiled at Celeste over the rim of the cup. If she had any hope of salvaging this meeting without this woman thinking she'd come completely unglued, she needed to stop thinking about Shep and weddings and falling in love, and start thinking about how she was going to get Ross Burris to agree to a one-on-one interview with Celeste Montgomery within the next few days. She could worry about dinner at Dalton's Grange later. Right now, she needed to get down to work.

She leaned back and tossed the cup in the garbage, then pushed her chair away from the table. "How would you like a tour of the arena, Celeste? Then after that, I'll give Ross a call, and we can get the ball rolling on your interview."

"That'd be great. Count me in."

Rylee followed Celeste out the door and into the long, air-conditioned corridor that led to the glass elevator. She began telling the other woman all about the convention center's state-of-the-art construction and how they expected it to bring in even more rodeo talent in the years to come. At least it was something to talk about. Something to keep her mind occupied.

But her heart was a lost cause.

Chapter Seven

"Mom, what's this all about?" Shep asked, looking at his watch. "I still need to shower before Rylee gets here."

"Just come with me for a minute. It won't take long."

Resisting the urge to sigh, Shep followed his mother up the staircase to the second floor, running his hand along the glossy wood railing as he went. He was tired and sweaty after bucking hay with Holt and Dale most of the afternoon, and his shoulders were aching. A long, hot shower sounded good. Followed by a cold beer and his mother's cooking. She'd been in the kitchen all day, making her spaghetti sauce from scratch. The rich, heavy scent filled the entire house, along with the smell of the homemade bread that was currently baking in the oven.

His stomach rumbled. He could almost taste the pasta, the warm, buttery bread and the salad with the tangy vinaigrette dressing that had been his grandmother's specialty. It was almost enough to make him forget that his entire family would be here tonight, grilling him and Rylee until long after the apple pie was served. Maybe he'd get lucky and they'd all be too busy eating to ask a ton of questions. But he wouldn't hold his breath.

His mom turned and gave him a smile over her shoulder. She was practically glowing, and Shep knew why. All her boys were just about married and settled down now. Her mind and heart were finally at ease.

Shep smiled back, feeling a now familiar stab of guilt. The thought of coming clean now, after all this, was almost too much to contemplate. His mom would be crushed. His dad and brothers would be pissed. And what about Rylee? What kind of fallout would be waiting for her? He knew she'd been worried about lying to Gabby, but what about her parents and her own brothers? It wouldn't be pretty. None of it would be.

Still, deep down, he knew that wasn't a good reason to get married. He was reckless, but he wasn't stupid. The thing driving him now was Rylee herself, and the temptation to have her for his own. He still believed they could make this work if she agreed to it. If they were lucky, everything else would fall into place eventually. And if they weren't? Well, he'd just have to deal with that when it happened.

He followed his mother into her bedroom, the late-afternoon sun slanting in warm rays of gold through the windows. Their cat, Steve, was stretched out in one of the sunbeams on the floor, all four paws in the air. He looked like roadkill. Shep nudged him with his boot as he passed, making sure he was still breathing. The cat chirped a meow and then closed his eyes again, too lazy to move.

"Now, don't feel any pressure to take this," Shep's mom said, walking over to her antique vanity and opening her jewelry box. "But I've been thinking about it since the other day, and in my heart, it just feels right to offer it. You and Grandma always had a special relationship…"

She pulled out a small velvet box and cracked it open. Inside was his grandmother's engagement ring. He re-

membered seeing it on her hand when he was little, sparkling against her papery skin. She'd told him the story of
when she and his grandpa had met dozens of times. She'd
been working at the movie theater in Tenacity when she
was only fifteen years old. His grandpa had driven by in
a convertible with his friends and had waved at her when
she was walking out the front doors. She'd smiled and
waved back, and he'd turned the car around so he could
ask her out. The rest was history. A love story for the ages.

He stared down at the ring now, suddenly overcome
with memories of her, with missing her and her wry sense
of humor. Her smiles, which were contagious. And her
hugs, which Shep had reveled in as the youngest of five
brothers, who got picked on more often than not. He could
remember running into her skirts and burying his face in
her apron when he was probably as young as three or four.
She'd been a huge part of his childhood, an important and
loving adult in his life. And he missed her terribly.

His mother watched him closely, probably trying to
gauge his interest in the ring. The fact that she would offer
this meant so much. But he had no idea if Rylee was even
going to marry him, let alone if she'd be interested in his
grandmother's ring.

"What are you thinking?" his mom asked softly.

Shep felt the muscles in his jaw bunch. His family
wasn't perfect, never had been. He'd been angry at his
dad for a long time, finding it hard to forgive him for
the way he'd treated his mother in the past. There'd been
cheating, lying, drunken foolishness back then. His dad
had changed and his parents still loved each other, despite everything. And they loved their sons with a deep
and fierce devotion that Shep had always felt to his bones.

He was lucky to be a Dalton. And if Rylee gave him the honor of becoming her husband, he knew she'd be welcomed into the family with the same love that he'd always known himself.

"I don't know what to say, Mom," he said, his voice low. "Thank you."

"Now, like I said, don't feel like you need to take it. But it's here if you want it. Grandpa had it custom-made in 1955, the year they were married. Just so you know."

Shep's grandfather had been a tough old cowboy with a gruff way about him. Except when it came to his wife, whom he'd doted on. Spoiled every day of her life. He wasn't surprised that a stock ring wouldn't have done for his pretty young bride with the raven curls.

Taking the box from his mother's hand, he took the ring out and held it up to the sunlight coming in through the window. There was one large square-cut diamond in the middle, surrounded by smaller diamonds all the way around. His mom had said it was old-fashioned the other day, but he thought it looked surprisingly contemporary. He guessed everything came back in style if you waited long enough. He wondered what kind of ring Rylee liked, what kind of style she preferred. She didn't wear much jewelry on a daily basis, only small earrings and a watch, but he thought the ring would look beautiful on her. But that wasn't a stretch. Everything looked good on Rylee.

He moved the ring back and forth, watching the diamonds create a prism of rainbow color in the vanity's mirror. "I still haven't talked to Rylee about her ring yet," he said. "Can I have a little time? I just want her to be happy with it. And I know she'd love this, but—"

"You don't have to explain. Take all the time you need. It'll be here."

Shep leaned down and kissed his mother on the cheek. She smiled, looking genuinely happy, genuinely pleased with this whole turn of events.

He thought about how his grandparents had met—the story of them waving to each other in the little town of Tenacity in the 1950s, when the world was simpler and their whole lives were ahead of them.

He swallowed hard. He thought about Rylee as a teenager and wondered if she ever thought they'd truly make good on that promise back then. And he wondered if someday, just maybe, they might tell the story of how they met, too.

Rylee looked down at her dress, something she'd found in the back of her closet and that she'd only worn once before. To a wedding, ironically. She remembered sitting in the back row feeling awkward and out of place. She'd barely known the bride, who'd been a work acquaintance, and she hadn't stayed for the reception. But she'd always loved the dress, a floral print that was flirty and sweet. Paired with her favorite cowboy boots, she thought it was the perfect thing to wear to the ranch for dinner.

She took a deep breath. This was it. The moment she'd been dreading for the last few weeks. Being in the same room with Shep's entire family and actually having to lie to their faces. Rylee hadn't been altogether sure she'd be able to do it when she woke up that morning. The thought of calling Shep and telling him that she didn't feel well had crossed her mind. It was true, she hadn't felt well. She'd been so nervous, her stomach had done somersaults when she'd stepped out of bed. But then he'd texted and said that his mother was making her famous all-day spaghetti sauce and was so happy about this dinner, and Rylee knew she'd just have to power through it.

She reminded herself again that Shep really did want to get married. And not only that—she was tempted to say yes. Which meant this was less like lying and more like…she wasn't sure really. But she knew that in order to get through tonight, she was going to have to put everything else on the back burner and simply wear a confident smile. What else could she do?

She lifted her hand now and rang the Dalton's doorbell with her heart in her throat. After a few seconds, it opened. She looked up to see Neal Dalton standing there, looking larger than life.

He smiled wide, and before she knew what was happening, he'd pulled her into a bear hug.

"Rylee!" he boomed. "It's so good to see you."

Rylee smiled against his denim shirt. He smelled like soap. Neal had always intimidated her a little. He used to be gruff, definitely quiet and on the broody side when she and Shep were kids. But he'd clearly grown a little softer around the edges since she'd seen him last. He was a grandfather now, with salt-and-pepper hair and a matching handlebar mustache, and she wondered if that had something to do with it.

"Hi, Mr. Dalton," she said, pulling away with a smile. "It's good to see you, too."

"Who's this Mr. Dalton fellow?" he asked with a wink. "It's going to be Dad soon enough. At least call me Neal."

"All right. Will do."

"Come in, come in."

He ushered her inside, where the house was bustling. There were a few little ones running around, and about a dozen adults visiting in the living room. The smell of warm bread wafted in from the kitchen and made Rylee's stomach growl, despite her nerves.

Everyone turned when she walked in the door and then made their way over one by one. Morgan, whom she hadn't seen in nearly as long as Neal, gave her a kiss on the cheek and introduced her to his wife, Erica, and their adorable, chubby-cheeked little girl, Josie. And then she was hugging Holt and meeting his wife, Amanda, and his son, Robby, Boone and his wife, Sofia, and Dale and his fiancée, Kendra, who owned one of the cutest bakeries in Bronco Heights, as well as her daughter, Mila, who was clutching a fat tabby cat in her arms.

By the time Shep came walking down the stairs, Rylee's head was spinning. There were so many of them. Such a big family. Honestly, not too much bigger than her own, but for some reason, things at Dalton's Grange felt larger than life, like Neal himself. Or maybe that was just the weight of the reality on her shoulders. When she and Shep told a few strangers they were engaged at Janet's party, she never would've imagined that lie would grow to be this large or intricate. She ran her palms down her dress as Shep came walking over.

"Hey, beautiful," he said, leaning down to give her a kiss.

At this point, it was hard to tell if that was for everyone else's benefit or her own. Regardless, she felt her knees grow weak, like they did every time he kissed her now. She wondered if her kisses had the same effect on him. She had to ask herself if he would ever love her, or if she was just a means to an end. It was unsettling. Especially now, as he pulled away and smiled down at her, his blue eyes twinkling.

"You made it. And in that dress, too. You look amazing."

He put his arm around her, and she leaned into his side, loving how solid he felt.

"I see you met all the significant others," he said. "And the offspring. Pretty cute, huh? Josie has everyone wrapped around her little finger, let me tell you. And Mila is our animal lover. She's more obsessed with the ranch than Dad is."

Rylee let her gaze fall on the little girl who was now sitting on the couch with the cat, stroking his head and talking to him in soft, gentle tones.

"She's a sweetheart," Rylee said. "It looks like she has a way with cats, too."

"Well, Steve is a bit of a narcissist, so he's all about the attention."

Rylee laughed. "I can't say I blame him."

Deborah came out of the kitchen wearing a lavender apron with ruffles around the bust and made a beeline for Rylee.

"Rylee! I hope you're hungry, honey," she said, taking her hand.

Rylee's stomach rumbled again. "I'm starving. Do you need some help in the kitchen?"

"Absolutely not. That's what Shep's dad is for. And dinner's almost ready anyway. Can we get you something to drink? A glass of wine, maybe?"

"Wine sounds wonderful."

"White or red? I think we have chardonnay and a pinot

noir that we bought at a local vineyard last summer. It's delicious."

At the mention of wine, Rylee remembered the chilled bottle in her fridge that she'd meant to bring as a gift. It probably wasn't as expensive as Deborah's, but it was a nice bottle. She'd completely forgotten, though, because she'd been so anxious leaving her apartment that evening.

"The pinot noir would be great," she said. "Thank you."

As if sensing her nerves, Shep tightened his arm around her waist. She could get used to this. They really did make a good team. He seemed to know when she needed him, and she liked to think the same was true about her. It didn't matter that they hadn't seen each other in years. They'd been able to pick right back up where they'd left off.

Deborah disappeared back into the kitchen, and Erica walked up and touched her arm.

"I just *love* your dress," the other woman said. "Where'd you get it?"

"Oh, thanks. I actually ordered it online for a wedding a few years ago. From an outlet that was going out of business, so it was on sale." Her cheeks warmed. Rylee had grown up thrifty. When you came from a family like hers, that had struggled making ends meet, you had to learn to be. She wasn't ashamed of it, but at the same time, she knew there was a good possibility Erica and her sisters-in-law shopped at more upscale places. Places that Rylee hadn't been able to afford before getting her promotion at the convention center.

"Oh, shoot," Erica said. "I wish they hadn't gone out of business. I'd be ordering one just like it."

"Do you even have room for another dress in your

closet?" This from Morgan, who was giving his wife a teasing look.

"You hush. There's tons of room in my closet."

"I love you, babe. But stretching the truth is your specialty. You're amazing at it."

Erica rolled her eyes, but there was obvious affection there. A playfulness that Rylee recognized in her relationship with Shep, too. Charm was something the Dalton men had in spades.

Deborah came in holding a glass of wine and handed it to Rylee with a smile. "Dinner will be ready in about ten minutes. You just make yourself at home, okay?"

"Thanks, Mrs. Dalton."

Rylee watched the other woman head back into the kitchen. For some reason, she couldn't stop calling them Mr. and Mrs. As if she was still in the eighth grade or something.

"Nervous?" Shep leaned down close to her ear so nobody else would hear. "You don't have to be, you know. They've always loved you."

"A little," she whispered back. "Aren't you?"

"I can handle them. I'm mostly worried about you. They can be a lot."

He'd always been protective of her, always wanting to shield her from anything that could hurt her. But this was different. This was his family. There was only so much shielding he could do. If they went ahead with this, if they went ahead and got married, she would have to hold her own, no matter what came at her. She'd be a Dalton.

At the thought of that, her stomach dipped.

Shep took her elbow and led her over to one of the big front windows. The view was gorgeous. You could see half the ranch from here, drenched in gold by the setting sun. In the distance, Black Angus cattle grazed, peppery specks against the emerald green pastures. Rylee took a sip of her wine, hardly able to believe she was standing here. That she was contemplating marriage to Shep. That Neal and Deborah might be her in-laws, and Dalton's Grange her eventual home. It was almost too much to absorb, even though she'd had several days to try and do just that.

"Hey," Shep said, gazing down at her. "Is everything okay?"

She nodded. She seemed to be getting asked that a lot lately. "Just thinking."

"About what?"

"You and me. All of this. I can't believe we're doing this."

"Pretending to be engaged? Or thinking about actually getting married?"

"Both."

Shep looked out the window, the muscles in his jaw working.

"What are you thinking about?" she asked, suddenly wanting to know more than anything.

He let his gaze settle on her again. "About whether or not you're going to go through with it."

Her heartbeat slowed. She wanted to go through with it. Who wouldn't want to marry Shep? But on the other hand, it'd be foolish not to consider the consequences. Which was a possibly ruined friendship. Or having to go through an annulment or a divorce and enduring all the talk that would follow. And there would be a lot of talk. Rylee was used to a certain amount of that—she'd grown up in claustrophobic Tenacity after all, and Tenacity was smaller than Bronco. But even so, people would have things to say, and she'd always hated being the subject of gossip. For someone who was shy and quiet by nature, it made her feel exposed and vulnerable. Like she needed to put up walls to defend herself. It felt like she'd done enough of that to last a lifetime.

"What do you say, Ry?" Shep asked, his voice low. "Are you going to marry me?"

It wasn't the proposal she'd always dreamed of. He wasn't on bended knee, holding out a ring. He hadn't professed his love, and neither had she.

"Shep," she began. "Do you love me?"

It was bold. Much bolder than she was used to being, but the stakes were too high now not to know.

He gazed down at her. She knew Shep better than most people did. But right then, she couldn't tell what he was thinking. His eyes were shuttered, revealing nothing. His mouth, normally tilting at one side with a ready smile, settled into a firm line, and her heart sank a little. Just a little. Because, really, she hadn't let herself hope for much more than the fleeting happiness of this fake engagement. If she did, if she let that hope in, she'd be risking pain in the end, and she cared too much about herself to let that happen.

So she continued looking up at him, her chin raised, her shoulders back.

"Rylee," he began. "I…"

She stood there, holding her breath. Whatever he was about to say, she'd be okay. They'd be okay. They were friends, and that was what mattered most in the end. And if she told herself that enough, maybe she'd even start to believe it.

"Dinner!" Deborah called from the kitchen. "Come and get it!"

Rylee exhaled shakily. But her stomach remained tight. Unable to relax because the answer she'd been waiting for hadn't materialized.

Boone walked up and smacked Shep on the shoulder. "Let's get after it, little brother."

Shep took her hand. A silent show of…what exactly? His skin was warm, rough against hers. She wanted to believe that he'd been about to tell her exactly what she wanted to hear. But she wasn't letting herself go there. She couldn't let herself go there.

So she walked into the kitchen beside him and put on her bravest face. Determined not to let anyone see how scared she was. Because, no matter what, no matter how she'd been spinning it to herself, she didn't just love Shep. She was in love with him. And that was the cold, hard truth.

"Rylee, have you thought about where you want to get married?" Sofia asked, handing the basket of garlic bread to Boone, who unloaded three pieces onto his overflowing plate.

Rylee had just taken a bite of her spaghetti and smiled awkwardly, her mouth full.

"Oh," Kendra said. "You guys should definitely get married out here. Can you picture it? A sunset wedding? The ranch always has the prettiest sunsets."

"No, you should one hundred percent get married at that new aquarium!" Mila said, a dot of spaghetti sauce on her chin. Rylee noticed that she liked to say "one hundred percent" a lot. A few minutes ago she'd told her mother that she one hundred percent wanted ice cream with her pie. "My friend Nellie's mom works out there, and she says people can rent it out, and then their family and kids get to visit for free and stuff."

"Honey, your chin," Kendra said. "No, I heard that, too." She turned back to Rylee. "It's not open to the public yet, but when it is, you can rent it out. And since that's where you guys reconnected, wouldn't it be romantic?"

"*Sooo* romantic," Erica said. "And what about your dress? Have you picked one out?"

"We don't even have a date yet," Shep said. "And can you guys let her finish chewing first before you continue with the grand spaghetti inquisition?"

Erica didn't seem to take offense at this. In fact, as far as Rylee could tell, they all treated each other like siblings. Teasing, joking, ribbing each other constantly. Something Rylee could appreciate, since she had brothers herself. She understood the dynamic. She liked the underlying playfulness in the room, the barely controlled chaos. It made her feel at home.

"You mean you don't know when you're gonna get married, Uncle Shep?" Mila said with a frown.

"Well, uh…" Shep looked over at Rylee.

"No, honey," Rylee said. "We're not quite sure yet."

"Oh, then you should one hundred percent get married at Christmas," Mila said with calm, eight-year-old conviction. "Then you'll get presents for getting married *and* presents for Christmas."

"That's an excellent idea, Mila," Shep said. "We'll one hundred percent consider that."

Erica pointed her fork at Rylee. "But the *dress*. Are you going to Ever After? I mean, you should. At least to window-shop. They have the most beautiful things, and Patrice is really wonderful about helping her brides pick out the dress of their dreams. It's a whole experience, believe me."

"Well, if you go," Deborah said, "and if you and your mother want company, I'd love to tag along. By the way, I've been wanting to call Norma, Rylee. Is it okay if I give her a ring? Shep wasn't sure if you'd had a chance to sit down and tell your parents about the engagement properly yet."

At the mention of her parents, Rylee had to force down a stubborn piece of garlic bread and almost choked on it. She'd been eating nonstop since they'd sat down at the table. She was too nervous to sit still.

She took a sip of her iced tea and then set it down again, almost knocking over Shep's in the process.

"I've talked to them," she said, clearing her throat. "I haven't been back to Tenacity since we got engaged, but we've talked over the phone…"

"I'm sure they're just thrilled their baby is getting married," Deborah said.

Rylee forced a smile. They were happy. But she also clearly remembered her mother's worry. If she and Shep were to call off their fake engagement tomorrow, her mom would probably be a little relieved, to tell the truth.

Her brothers, of course, had reacted in the typical big-brother way. *If he hurts you, we're going to kill him* type thing. Deep down, they were teddy bears, and they'd always loved Shep, so she wasn't that worried about them, but even so, they were probably going to pull him aside at some point and threaten him with his life, which wasn't going to be pleasant.

Josie began wiggling in her high chair, and Erica got up to clean her face and lift her out. The little girl was so cute, looking up at her mother with such adoration, her chubby little cheeks stained with spaghetti sauce.

"Have you thought about a wedding planner?" Erica asked, bringing Josie back to the table and plopping her down on her lap. "I guess you might not need one if it's small and intimate…"

Boone laughed. "Small and intimate? This family?"

Shep gave Rylee an apologetic look. It was a lot. But at the same time, she couldn't help but enjoy it a little, too. Deep down, she felt like a princess. Which was why so many little girls dreamed of this moment practically from birth. The ring, the dress, the venue, the groom… It was all very sweet and magical.

And nerve-racking.

"What do you think?" she asked Shep. "Small and intimate?"

"I don't care. Just as long as you show up."

He winked at her. That familiar, mischievous wink that was so very Shep, and all of a sudden everything else fell away. His family, the dinner, all the worries about how they'd let it get this far, and she gazed over at him. *As long as you show up…*

Was that what she was going to do? Marry him?

She still wasn't sure.

Chapter Eight

Shep pulled up to BH247, his truck's motor rumbling through the cool night air. He had his window cracked, and he breathed in the scent of the asphalt, of the tidy rows of spring flowers planted out front. So different from the smells of the ranch—the warm smell of hay and animals. Of grass and wood and leather.

He looked over at Rylee, her profile bathed in shadow. She had her hands tucked neatly in her lap, and his denim jacket wrapped around her shoulders. She'd had a couple of glasses of wine, so he'd wanted to drive her home, just to be safe. He'd bring her car back into town tomorrow.

She turned to him, her eyes dark and lovely. Her heart-shaped lips glistening in the gritty light.

"Thank you for such a nice dinner," she said. "Your mom went to so much trouble. I can't imagine feeding that many people on the regular."

"She likes it. She says cooking is her love language. I mean, eating is my love language, but whatever."

She laughed. "Well, she's really good at it. That bread alone…"

"I know." He patted his stomach. "If I wasn't trying to save room for pie, I would've eaten like…well, like Boone."

"Where does he *put* it all?"

"He works it off. Ranching burns a ton of calories."

"And your six-pack is proof."

"Are you trying to say I have a nice body, Rylee?" He flexed and kissed one of his biceps.

"You're a tease."

"Oh, I beg to differ. I'd give you anything you wanted. All you have to do is ask."

He said this playfully, but if she only knew how serious he really was...

They sat there for a minute, a charged silence settling between them. Outside the truck's cracked window, Shep could hear crickets chirping their midnight melody. In the distance, a couple of dogs barked, and beyond that, cars passed on the highway.

Rylee pulled at a thread on her dress then looked over at him in the darkness. "Do you want to come in?" she asked. "For a cup of coffee?"

His heart thumped out a steady rhythm inside his chest. It had been a long time since anyone had affected him like this. Made his heart pound and his palms damp. Just sitting beside her in the cab of the truck had him jumping with anticipation. With excited nerves.

"One hundred percent," he said.

She laughed again, and the sound warmed him through. He liked making her laugh. He liked making her smile. But most of all, he liked when she looked at him like she was looking at him now. Like she might feel the same.

His jaw muscles tightened then, as he pictured how she'd looked earlier tonight. When she'd asked if he loved her. He'd literally frozen. He hadn't known how to answer. And then he hadn't had to answer at all because his mother had called everyone to dinner just in time.

She watched him, probably wondering why he'd grown so quiet all of a sudden. But he kept thinking about that question. And the fact that he hadn't known how to answer—because the answer wasn't that simple. At least, it wasn't for Shep.

Love had always been a complicated word for him. Entangled with the likes of *responsibility* and *commitment*. Both of which he knew nothing about, since he'd grown up looking to his father as an example. Neal Dalton had turned out to be a terrible one, cheating on his wife, breaking her trust, hurting his kids by association. He'd worked hard over the years to make it up to his family, and his wife had forgiven him. But for Shep, there'd been lasting damage. He now had a skewed idea of commitment and responsibility. Both those things were fragile; they could be shattered if you had clumsy hands. He was scared of hurting anyone the way his mother had been hurt. The way he'd been hurt, too. He didn't want to mess anything up, and the easiest way to do that was by not letting himself feel the deep stuff. The scary stuff. The stuff that could actually change him as a person, if he let it.

So...did he love her? He wasn't sure he could answer that question, even now. Even though Rylee deserved an answer. He was asking her to marry him, for God's sake. And he couldn't even let himself utter the word *love*, for fear of falling from this emotional tightrope he'd been walking.

He cut the engine, and Rylee opened her door. He opened his, too, and stepped out into the cool night air, the breeze ruffling his hair. He hadn't worn his hat tonight. He'd actually combed his hair neatly and had worn a starched white shirt. He'd spent the last three hours feeling like an accountant, with the collar itchy against his neck. But Rylee seemed to like it. She'd told him twice that he looked handsome, and he'd caught her a few times watching him from across the room. So it didn't matter if the collar was itchy, or if he looked like he was getting ready to do someone's taxes. She thought he looked good, and that was all that mattered. Maybe he'd have to get out of his ranch clothes more often.

He followed her up the steps to her apartment, trying to be a gentleman and not let his gaze roam all over her backside, but he was failing miserably. She was so beautiful, he not only wanted to let his gaze roam, he wanted to let his hands roam, too. She only seemed to have grown more attractive as the days passed, as he got to know her better as an adult. She was a stunning woman, inside and out.

Stopping in front of her door, she dug her keys out of her purse.

"It's a good thing everyone thinks we're engaged," she said. "Or this would be a scandal in the morning."

"Why's that?"

"Because everyone knows everyone else's business at BH247. We're probably being watched as we speak."

Honestly, he didn't mind all of Bronco knowing he was being invited into Rylee Parker's apartment, engaged or not. If the rumor mill had him hooking up with a woman like her, he could definitely live with that.

She unlocked the door and stepped inside to turn on the light. He followed her in and looked around. He'd never been to her place before. It was neat as a pin and decorated in soft, feminine colors. The pastel throw pillows on the cream-colored sectional reminded him of Easter eggs. The entire place smelled like cinnamon. There was a big bookcase beside the TV full of hardcovers and paperbacks, little knickknacks and framed photos of family and friends.

He stepped closer to look at them.

"I'll go put the coffee on," she said, shrugging out of her coat. "Be right back."

He smiled over his shoulder, then turned back to the pictures. There was one of her in a black cap and gown on her college graduation day. Norma and Lionel were on either side of her, beaming proudly. He remembered them coming to visit his parents at the ranch when he was little, and him getting to play with their sweet daughter, something he'd always looked forward to. There was another picture of her as a toddler, sitting on a countertop in a flower-print swimsuit, holding a phone to her ear. She'd been such a cute little kid, her auburn hair hanging in silky ringlets around her face. But it was the photo next to that one that just about stopped his heart. It was of him and Rylee as preteens on her old gelding, Tuff. Shep was sitting behind her with his arms around her waist, and she had her head thrown back in a laugh. His father had taken this picture, the moment frozen forever in time.

He stood there staring at it, letting himself be transported back to that summer day. He could almost feel Tuff's warmth underneath his legs, the horse's musky scent on his cutoff shorts. He could remember how it felt to be so close to Rylee back then, almost like they were the same person, one an extension of the other. He remembered how it felt to wrap his arms around her, wanting to keep her close and safe. He could hardly believe they'd fallen out of touch like they had. That he'd let himself go a month, let alone twelve years, without tracking her down. What in the world was wrong with him?

But deep down, he knew the answer. He'd known that if he found Rylee again, it wouldn't just be a simple reunion between two old friends. It would go further than that, be much more meaningful. And he'd been right, hadn't he? He'd actually brought up that promise they'd made to each other when they'd been teenagers on the brink of the rest of their lives. He'd brought it up, and he'd gotten her to go along with it.

And now, he was in deep. Very, very deep. What started out as a light, playful lie had turned into a burning desire that he wasn't quite sure what to do with, even now. Because if it wasn't light and playful anymore, then it would have to mean something. It would have to mean a lot.

Up until now, until he'd seen this faded picture in front of him, he'd been able to fool himself into thinking he could handle the repercussions. He'd been able to talk his way out of anything, even his true feelings for Rylee, whatever those turned out to be. But now… Now he knew there was no talking himself out of anything anymore.

"My favorite picture of us." She came up beside him and hooked her arm in his. "We were so young. Can you believe how innocent we were?"

"Well, you were. Not so sure about me."

She laughed. "You did corrupt me a little."

"A *little*?"

"Believe me, I wanted you to."

He turned to look down at her, and she immediately looked away. The light in her apartment was dim, but he could see that she was blushing furiously.

She chewed her bottom lip, still avoiding his gaze because she'd always been shy like this. He saw her pulse flutter in that delicate hollow at the base of her throat. It tapped like moth wings there, tempting him to bend close and kiss it. To feel her warmth and vitality underneath his mouth.

And then, finally, she looked up at him. Held his gaze with a new confidence he wasn't sure he'd seen before. And maybe that was because she knew she had him in the palm of her hand. He would've done anything for Rylee right then. Anything she asked him to.

"The coffee will be ready soon," she said.

"I don't want coffee."

"What do you want?"

"You have to know." It wasn't exactly a romantic declaration, but Shep wasn't exactly a romantic kind of guy. At least, he'd never been before. He'd been told he was a good time, that he was charming. But he'd never been told that he was particularly romantic. He said what he felt at the moment and wasn't used to sugarcoating anything. Rylee knew that better than most people.

Still, he wished he had the courage to say what was in his heart right then. That he didn't just want her, but he needed her. He was starting to need her in a way that had him spooked, quite frankly.

"You know," she said. "I think back to Janet's party, and how I felt when I saw you again after all this time…"

He swallowed hard. "And how's that?"

"Relieved, almost." She frowned. "Does that sound strange?"

"No. I think I know what you mean. For me, it was like I'd been missing something. And I finally got it back. So *relieved* is a good way to put it."

She nodded, looking far away for a second. He reached up and touched her hair, moved it away from her face until her gaze met his again.

"And then when we decided to get the necklace back—" She stopped short, and her eyes widened.

"What?"

"Oh my God. Shep…"

"What is it?"

"I completely forgot. I still have the necklace. *Here.* I have it here! I forgot to take it back to the mayor."

He laughed. "Uh-oh. Better late than never? That's okay, his wife will just be happy to have it back."

"I know. It's so pretty."

"It is pretty, but a necklace like that is nothing without a beautiful woman wearing it."

She gazed up at him, her lashes long and dark. Her lips parted slightly. That spot at the base of her throat, tempting him more than ever.

"I'd like to see you wearing it," he finished. "And nothing else."

The room suddenly grew so still, so quiet, that he could hear the blood rushing in his ears.

Rylee continued looking up at him, her lovely eyes taking him in. All of him. There was no hiding anything from her anymore, and he wondered if she knew how he actually felt about her now. If she could see through all his crap, down to the bones of everything.

Slowly, she stepped forward. Then reached up and put her arms around his neck. She pressed herself against him, and it was like the other night when they'd danced at Doug's. Except now, they were the only ones in the room. There was no thumping music, no bustling crowd.

No sound at all except for the soft inhale and exhale of her breath and that rushing in his ears.

Moving her hair away from her neck, he leaned down and kissed it softly, feeling her shiver underneath his lips. He'd kissed Rylee lots of times since the night of Janet's party. But tonight, it felt different. It felt real, genuine. Like these kisses weren't meant to convince anyone of anything.

Rylee tilted her head all the way back, and he moved his lips up her throat, kissing along her jawline. He breathed in the sweet scent of her perfume. He felt her tremble in his arms, felt her sway when he took her earlobe in his teeth.

"Are we doing what I think we're doing?" she whispered.

"What do you think we're doing?"

"I think you're about to spend the night."

"I think you might be right."

He knew it was a risk they were taking. Their friendship was on the line, and that was no small thing. Sleeping together would change everything. But the question was, would it change it for the better...or the worse?

He slid his hand from the small of her back, down the curve of her bottom, and heard her breath catch in her throat.

He wanted to sweep her into his arms, carry her to the bedroom and close the door behind them. He wanted to lay her on the bed and unzip her dress. He wanted to hear her say his name, over and over again, until she was too lost in pleasure to say anything else.

But he didn't move an inch, even though every nerve ending in his body was humming. He just stood there because he knew how important this moment was. He didn't want her choosing him now and regretting it later. Of course, there was no guarantee she wouldn't regret it later, even if they stood here all night long. But he wanted to hear her say she wanted this, too. He wanted to hear her say that because if she didn't, he'd always wonder, and he didn't think he could live with that.

"Are you sure, Rylee?"

For a few agonizing seconds, he wondered if she might say no. And then what would he do? He knew what he'd do. He'd go home and take a cold shower, and nurse what was left of his heart. It wouldn't be easy, but that was what he'd do because Rylee came first. She'd always come first.

And then, miraculously, she nodded. But her brows were furrowed. There was a tiny wrinkle between them as she gazed up at him.

"What about you, Shep?" she asked. "Are *you* sure?"

It was a simple question, yet had so many implications. He was sure. In some ways, he was more sure of this than of anything else in his life. But he'd be lying if he said those implications didn't worry him plenty.

"I'm sure," he said. It was all he could manage right then.

And it was all she apparently needed. She put her hands on either side of his face, then stood on her tiptoes and pressed her lips to his.

He could feel the eagerness there. The hunger.

Then, in one swift motion, he swept her up in his arms like he'd been dying to do for the last half an hour. He bounced her a couple of times against his chest, making her laugh. His heart hammered at the sound. At the feel of her weight in his arms. Slight, yet so very significant.

"Now," he said with a wink. "Let's go find that necklace."

* * *

Rylee had been dreaming. A wonderful dream that had given her butterflies. They lingered in her belly now, with the early morning light staining the insides of her closed eyelids orange.

She lay there, still and quiet, afraid to move for fear the details of the dream would fade like dreams so often did. She'd been dancing with Shep. But not in a crowded bar with people all around. They'd been dancing at their wedding. She could still hear the music from the live band in her ears. Or maybe it was still in her heart—thumping, thumping, thumping.

She felt her lips tilt into a smile. But this time, it wasn't because of the dream. It was because she'd started remembering something else altogether. Something that was coming back into sharp clarity. Sparkling in her mind and flashing in beautiful bursts of rainbow color.

She and Shep had spent the night together. And it had been wonderful. He'd been gentle and sweet and intuitive about what she'd wanted in a way that had left her breathless and shaking in his arms.

She turned her face into the softness of her pillow now and let her eyes flutter open to the light coming in through the blinds. In a minute, she'd roll over and curl into his naked side. She'd kiss his shoulder and move her leg over his and feel those rough little hairs tickle her skin.

But for the next few seconds, she wanted to savor the moment. This moment when she felt so excited about the future, whatever that might be. She wanted to soak it all in, until it saturated her completely, and so she'd remember how it felt to be truly happy for the first time in a while.

She took a deep, even breath. And then rolled over to kiss him good morning.

"Shep—"

She barely got his name out before her heart, which had been beating so lightly a minute before, sank like a stone inside her chest.

His side of the bed was empty. The sheets were cold and rumpled. She reached out to touch them and then recoiled without being able to help it.

Maybe he was in the bathroom? Or the kitchen, making them a cup of coffee? But judging by the thick, ominous silence that had settled over the apartment, it was clear he wasn't in either of those places. He was definitely gone.

Rylee bit the inside of her cheek. She felt cheap. This, despite all the warm feelings that had surrounded her only a minute ago. She'd never had a one-night stand before. She'd never slept with anyone and then woken up to find them gone. Shep had to have known how this would make her feel. He had to have known that...

Trying not to jump to conclusions, she pulled the sheets up to her chest and reached for her phone. Maybe there'd been some kind of emergency and he'd texted after he'd left. Maybe she'd slept right through it. She knew she was grasping at straws, but she couldn't help it.

Her heart sank when she saw there were no text notifications. She sat there for a minute, her eyes stinging.

She and Shep didn't know each other very well as adults yet, and she absolutely didn't know how he usually acted after sex. But this was so strange, so out of character, that she shook her head, for absolutely nobody's benefit but her own. As if to convince herself there was something she was missing.

After a few seconds, she scooted over to his side of the bed and moved the blankets out of the way. And sure enough, there was a note on the nightstand. She'd almost missed it because it was tucked underneath a coaster.

She reached for it and opened it up. It wasn't until right then that she noticed her hands were trembling.

Have to get back for the morning feeding. —Shep

Rylee sat there staring at it as if it were written in a foreign language. She pulled in a breath and let it out slowly. Then took another and another, until she felt herself relax some.

Okay. So, it wasn't exactly an emergency. But it was a completely logical reason to have to leave early. Still, those words were so curt. Like something he'd tell an acquaintance, not a woman he'd just spent the night with.

Frowning, she put the note back on the nightstand. She was so confused. Was he regretting their night together? She didn't want to read into anything, but it was hard not to. Suddenly, what she wanted most was to call Gabby. To tell her best friend what had happened and get her take on this. Gabby had grown so wise about these things, where Rylee felt inexperienced and naive in comparison.

Despite trying to hold them back, tears filled her eyes anyway. But she couldn't tell Gabby anything, could she? Because Gabby didn't even know the truth about her relationship with Shep. Or why this would be such a big deal in the first place. As far as Gabby was concerned, they were actually engaged—had been this entire time—and him leaving this morning wouldn't mean anything except he had cows to feed.

The guilt from keeping this from her best friend was suddenly so overwhelming that she put her face into her hands and began sobbing like a little kid.

It wasn't just Gabby that she'd deceived. It was her parents. It was Shep's parents. And her brothers and his, too. It was everybody that they knew, and it didn't really matter if they actually ended up getting married or not, their loved ones had still been lied to.

Rylee thought she could handle straightening things out with her family if it came to that. But right then, she didn't think she could keep this secret one minute longer from the woman she'd grown the closest to since moving to Bronco. Rylee shared everything with Gabby. It was time she shared this, too.

She just hoped their friendship would survive it.

Chapter Nine

Shep drove into the early morning sunlight with his dark aviator sunglasses on and the truck's visor down. He had a splitting headache, despite the two Tylenol he'd taken after leaving Rylee's apartment.

He guessed it was the beer with dinner. Or all the salt in the spaghetti? Or maybe he'd finally woken up to the fact that this whole engagement caper was a hell of a lot more serious than he'd given it credit for. Because the way he felt about Rylee was no longer something he could push to the back burner. It could no longer be treated like some game, engineered for the sole purpose of entertaining him and giving him what he wanted. There were real feelings here. And very real consequences.

He gritted his teeth and felt his jaw muscles tighten almost painfully. Before last night, he could've seen himself falling in love with Rylee. Of course he could. In the future. If everything worked out the way he hoped. After all, falling in love with her would be easy. He was already halfway there. But last night, the second he'd laid her down on the bed and looked into her eyes, he knew that moment was already here, whether he was ready for it or not.

Now, driving back to Dalton's Grange this morning, his

hands in a death grip on the steering wheel, all he could think about was the fact that he *wasn't* ready. Because the reality of it, of her, felt like a lightning bolt to his heart. He'd been so stupid. So damn stupid for thinking that he could orchestrate this like some kind of movie. That no matter how it would end, it would be on a positive note. That they'd always be friends, no matter what.

The fact was he was in love with her. And honestly, from the depths of his soul, he didn't know how to be in love like this. He didn't know how to let her in, where she absolutely needed to be. He'd always assumed that when this kind of love happened, if it happened, he'd know how to navigate it.

And now, here he was. So freaked out that he'd thrown off the covers this morning, quietly and like a total coward, and had tiptoed out the door holding his boots so he wouldn't wake her.

Frowning, he stared at the road ahead. He'd left a note. But just barely. The list of things he *should've* said was practically endless. *I love you. I've always loved you. There's never been another woman who's made me feel like this, and I don't know that I can live without you now.*

Of course, he couldn't say any of those things because admitting them to himself was hard enough. Admitting them to her? Impossible. Or at least, that was how it felt now as he continued grinding his teeth and gripping the steering wheel.

So he'd left that stupid note and had hoped she'd accept it for what it looked like. That he'd been in a hurry. And maybe that he was a little bit of an insensitive brute, but a mostly well-meaning one. He just needed to buy himself some time. But what exactly for? What was he going to do when he got back to the ranch?

He already knew what he was going to do. He was going to throw himself into physical labor and try to forget about this feeling unfurling inside his chest. He needed to put some distance between himself and Rylee Parker. He wouldn't let himself think of how rotten that would look to her. Hell, how rotten it would actually *be*. This was self-preservation, plain and simple.

He reached over to where his phone lay in the passenger seat and clicked off the ringer. He just needed some time. That was all. He just needed some time to figure this out.

Rylee sat across from Gabby at a small table at Wild Willa's Saloon. Usually they sat at the famous Get Lucky Bar, which was shaped like a four-leaf clover. But tonight, they'd chosen a quieter spot in the corner where they'd be able to talk.

The drinks at Wild Willa's were good, but the ambience was better. It was a fun place to come after work or on the weekends. When Rylee and Gabby met here, they'd talk about their jobs, their mutual acquaintances, Ryan… Poor Ryan was a frequent and favorite topic of conversation.

Gabby took a sip of her lemon drop martini and licked the sugar from her lips.

"Mmm," she said. "That's *so* good. Best lemon drop around."

Rylee had one in front of her, too, but she hadn't touched it yet. She'd been too busy rehearsing what she was going to say. How she'd try to explain it in a way that made sense. But honestly, she expected Gabby to be angry. Really angry. And hurt, too. Rylee would be, if it were her.

Gabby set her martini down and leaned her elbows on the table. "Okay. Out with it. You've been acting weird all day. Did something happen between you and Shep?"

At the mention of Shep's name, Rylee's heart twisted. He'd sent a brief text yesterday, but hadn't called since they'd slept together. Which was hurtful and more than a little dismissive. She hadn't tried calling him because her defenses were up now. If he wanted to talk, he knew where to find her. Until then, she wasn't going to go chasing him like a lovesick teenager.

Swallowing hard, she tapped the base of her glass. This wasn't going to be easy. But she knew she'd feel better after confessing to Gabby. She needed her friend right now, and if she had to take a few lumps, that was okay. She deserved them.

"Something did happen between me and Shep, but that's not what I wanted to talk to you about…"

Gabby sat up straighter. "Is everything okay?"

"I'm just worried you're going to hate me."

"I could never hate you. Whatever it is."

"You say that now…"

Gabby watched her, a little wrinkle forming between her brows. Somebody had put some money in the jukebox across the room, and it began playing a Garth Brooks song that had been one of Rylee's favorites in high school. It reminded her of Shep and the river and being sunburned and happy. Those had been good times. The best times. Things got so complicated when you got older. She wondered if anyone had ever explained that to her when she was a kid. If they had, she hadn't paid enough attention to remember. When you were seventeen, the thought of turning thirty might as well be like turning eighty. It was too far beyond comprehension, too far beyond the young, tender frontal lobe that only cared about boys and pizza and romance novels. At least, that was how it had been for Rylee.

She looked over at Gabby now and licked her lips. Hoping her friend would understand this. And would forgive her.

"Remember Janet Halstead's birthday party?"

"The one in Wonderstone Ridge?"

Rylee nodded.

"The one where you got engaged," Gabby said. "How could I forget that?"

Rylee's stomach dipped. It was now or never. If she didn't come clean soon, she was going to lose her nerve altogether.

"Well, kind of," she said. "We *kind of* got engaged."

Gabby frowned. "What do you mean?"

"You know that Shep and I grew up together. We were best friends until I left for college in California…"

"Yeah, I knew that. And he was your first crush."

"He was."

Gabby waited, putting her chin in her hand. She probably thought this was the most boring story ever.

Rylee cleared her throat. "Well, when I drove over to his place to say goodbye that day, the day I left for college, we made each other a promise."

"Oh?"

"A promise that if we weren't married by the time we turned thirty, we'd marry each other."

"Wait a minute," Gabby said. "You got engaged because of a promise you made when you were teenagers?"

"Yes. No. Kind of."

"Rylee, you're not making any sense."

"I know. And when I tell you the whole story, you're probably going to be even more confused."

"Try me."

Taking a deep breath, Rylee plowed on. "We made each other that promise. But when we met up at Janet's party, we hadn't seen each other since that day."

"And you decided to make good on it?" Gabby snapped her fingers. "Just like that?"

"Not exactly. We were standing in this crowd, and one thing led to another, and Shep kissed me." Rylee's heartbeat kicked up a notch, and all of a sudden, her sweater felt too warm. "Everyone saw and started clapping, and Shep, well... You'd have to know how much he likes to joke around. He jokes all the time. I think it's how he deals with things. He jokes about them, and they don't seem as real. Or as serious."

Gabby nodded.

"Well, he told everyone he was just giving his new fiancée a kiss. Because of that promise, he said we were engaged. But of course, they all thought we really *were* engaged, because why wouldn't they? We'd had a few drinks, and we got caught up in it. Everyone was so sweet and excited for us, and we didn't think it would go beyond that party. Beyond that room."

"Rylee," Gabby said slowly. "Are you trying to tell me that you were pretending that night?"

Rylee grazed her bottom lip with her teeth. "Yes."

"And are you telling me that you've been pretending this whole time?"

"I'm so sorry, Gabby. But yes."

Leaning back, Gabby shook her head. "But why? Why would you do that?"

"I don't have a great explanation, except that we didn't think it would ever get this far. At first, it was just a fun thing to do. Kind of like when we were kids, something we'd laugh about later. And the next morning, I got your text, and we realized word had already gotten around. That our families probably knew. Our parents. Shep's mom has been on him to settle down for so long, he thought maybe we could just go along with it for a few weeks and then break up, and then that would be that."

"You mean have a fake breakup." Gabby crossed her arms over her chest, giving Rylee a flat look from across the table.

"Yes. That."

"And then what?"

"And then...and then we started spending time to-gether, and Shep started talking about actually getting married. For real."

Gabby rubbed her temple. Not unlike a mother who was exasperated with her teenage daughter. "*Why* in the hell didn't you tell me any of this? I feel like a complete jerk now. I was trying to get you to try on wedding dresses!"

"I know. I'm sorry, Gabby. I didn't say anything at first because it was such a secret, and I didn't want to put you in the position of having to keep it from Ryan. Or risk Bella overhearing us. Or... I don't know. So many things. And then one day turned into two days. And then two weeks, and it got harder and harder to tell you the truth. I was so worried you'd be mad. And you have every right to be."

Gabby sighed and took a sip of her martini. And then another, before putting it down again. "Well, I'm not thrilled. But I'm not *mad*. I just wish you'd trusted me with it. But you're right. I would've wanted to tell Ryan, so there's that…"

Rylee gave her friend a small smile. Maybe it would be okay after all. Having things unsettled with Shep was bad enough. She didn't think she could handle it if she and Gabby weren't speaking.

"So," Gabby continued, "Shep actually wants to get married for real?"

Rylee nodded.

"That's so romantic. He must've fallen head over heels for you, Rylee."

"I don't know. He hasn't said so. He just keeps saying how practical it is, how much it makes sense. I'm so confused."

"But you love him." It wasn't a question. Gabby knew how Rylee felt about Shep.

"I do."

"Then what are you going to do?"

"Getting married would be ridiculous…wouldn't it?"

Gabby shrugged. "I don't know. It's not like you haven't known each other your entire lives. You're friends, and that's half the battle right there. It could be a huge adventure."

"Or a huge mistake."

"But you won't know until you make it."

"True…" Rylee paused, running her hands over the tabletop. "There's something else I need to tell you."

"Oh Lord. I don't know if I can take any more surprises."

"Well, this just happened. So I haven't kept it from you. You're actually the first to know."

Gabby smiled and sat up a little straighter, clearly happy with this turn of events. "Spill."

"We slept together the other night. For the first time."

Gabby's smile stretched wider. She was always beautiful, but when she smiled, she was truly stunning. "Oh, Ry. I'm so happy for you."

Suddenly, and without warning, Rylee's eyes filled with tears.

"Oh no," Gabby said, reaching for her hand from across the table. "What happened? What did he do? Am I going to have to kill him? Because I will, you know."

"No, it's nothing like that." But even as she said it, Rylee knew it *was* something like that. Shep was ghosting her; it was becoming more and more obvious. She didn't know why, but she had to assume the reason was significant. She had to wonder if this had been a mistake for him. Not just sleeping together, but maybe this entire engagement thing. Maybe he was finally realizing that getting married was bananas. Not an adventure like Gabby just said. But just plain bananas.

"Well," Gabby said. "What is it then?"

"He hasn't called. We haven't talked since."

Gabby's expression grew chilly. "I see. I *am* going to have to kill him."

"Don't kill him," Rylee said, trying for a note of levity. "That would get messy, and I can't have my bestie going to jail. Who'd give me outfit advice?"

"Nice try, but I know you're heartbroken about this."

Rylee wiped her eyes. "Maybe a little. But Shep has always been awful at communication. He probably just needs time. And I can give that to him."

"Don't give him too much time. There are a lot of guys who would love to be with you, Rylee. Don't forget that."

Rylee squeezed her friend's hand. Even if that were true, she didn't want anyone else. She wanted Shep. She wanted what she'd dreamed about the other night—the wedding, the life, the happiness. She wanted the fairy tale. But there was one glaring problem with fairy tales.

They weren't reality.

Shep stepped up to Rylee's door and took a deep breath. There was a good chance she wouldn't be thrilled to see him. After all, he hadn't warned her he was coming. He'd been in town at the feed store and had decided to stop by on his way back to the ranch. They hadn't talked in a few days. Actually, since the night they'd spent together, and he knew it was way past time. If she didn't tell him to go straight to hell, that is. That was always a possibility.

He stood there on her doorstep with a ton of excuses running through his head. *I've been swamped*, or *I've been sick*. Things that would hold water, or were at least halfway true, and would let him avoid the *whole* truth. Which was, *I'm scared*...

Taking his Stetson off, he ran a hand through his hair. He probably smelled like horses. He should've planned this better. But he knew if he'd given himself time to think about it, he would've kept on driving.

Rylee deserved better than what he'd been giving her. But he was so terrified of screwing it all up that he'd just been stuck these last few days. Anxious about moving forward, but not wanting to move back, either. Even his mother had noticed something was wrong, but she hadn't come right out and asked, and he hadn't offered. This was how Shep dealt with issues in his life. Always had. He kept them to himself, and he figured them out on his own. Period.

But the thing was, standing here now, he knew it was time to talk. It was true, he didn't know what he was going to say, and maybe when he opened his mouth, it would be a shock to them both. But if he didn't at least try, he was going to lose her for good. He knew that without a doubt, and he couldn't let that happen.

Steeling himself, he raised his hand and knocked. And then waited with his heart tapping in his throat.

After a few seconds, he heard footsteps. Then a pause, as she presumably looked through the peephole.

When the door finally opened, he realized he was holding his breath.

"Shep," she said coolly.

She had her hair pulled into a high ponytail and was wearing a white T-shirt and jeans with holes in the knees. She looked so effortlessly beautiful that for a second all he could do was stare.

"What are you doing here?" she continued, not slamming the door in his face, but not inviting him in, either.

He looked down at his boots, knowing that all the excuses he'd been contemplating a minute ago weren't going to cut it. But the truth wasn't a possibility, either. At least, not right this minute. He needed… Hell, he didn't know what he needed. He was a mess was what he was.

"It's Saturday, so I came into town to get some grain," he said, "and thought I'd stop by to say hi."

She watched him, obviously wary. "Hi."

"I know we haven't talked. Since…"

"Since sleeping together?" she finished flatly.

Ouch. She wasn't going to make this easy. Then again, he deserved everything she'd throw at him and more.

"I'm sorry about that," he said, pinching the brim of his Stetson between his thumb and forefingers. Trying not to come undone by the scent of her perfume in the air. "I guess I wasn't ready for how all this would make me feel."

That part wasn't a lie, at least. He hadn't been ready. In fact, he'd been so unprepared, this whole thing had damn well knocked him flat on his ass.

"And how's that?" Rylee asked, narrowing her eyes at him.

"Confused."

"That makes two of us."

All he wanted was to step forward and pull her into his arms, where she fit so perfectly. He wanted to kiss that hollow in her throat and breathe her in and feel her body warm next to his. But by the way she was eyeing him, he wasn't sure that would be welcome. Maybe it wouldn't be welcome ever again, and he realized that by being so afraid of screwing everything up, he might've gone ahead and screwed it up anyway.

"Can I come in?" he asked.

She waited, looking like she was thinking it over. Probably weighing her options. Shove him down the steps or offer him a cup of coffee. The jury was still out on that one.

After a few seconds, she stepped quietly aside and motioned him inside.

He stepped past, feeling the tension crackle between them. It was almost palpable.

She closed the door behind him, and when he turned

around, she had her arms crossed over her chest. *Nope.* She definitely wasn't going to make this easy.

"How have you been?" he asked. Then immediately wanted to suck the words back in.

"Fine. How have you been?"

He ran a frustrated hand through his hair. This wasn't going how he'd planned. But then again, he hadn't actually planned it, had he? Maybe if he'd start thinking about things before jumping right into them, he wouldn't find himself in situations like this.

The problem was this wasn't just an awkward encounter with someone he probably wouldn't see again any time soon. This was Rylee. His Rylee. He had to make this right, but he wasn't sure how. For maybe the first time in his life, his charm, which he'd always relied so heavily on, was failing him miserably.

"I know you're upset," he said. "And I don't blame you."

"Why would I be upset?"

Heat crept up his neck, and he shifted uncomfortably on his feet. "I'm sorry I haven't called."

At that, she just stood there. It was hard to tell what she was thinking. Her expression was shuttered. *She* was shuttered. She obviously didn't want to give him the opportunity to hurt her any more than he already had, and all of a sudden he felt like an absolute idiot. Sure, this whole thing had taken him by surprise, and he was scared to death, to be honest. But he did know he never should've left that morning. He never should've left her, period.

"Rylee—"

But before he could say anything more, his phone rang from his pocket.

"Sorry," he mumbled, pulling it out to see Boone's name flash across the screen.

Rylee continued gazing up at him, and he thought about not answering, but there was always the possibility it was an emergency. Ever since his mother's heart attack a few years ago, he had a hard time ignoring calls from his family.

Holding up a finger, he gave her an apologetic look. "One second, promise."

"It's okay."

He pressed the accept button. "Hello?" he bit out.

"Jeez," Boone said. The reception was crackly, and wind buffeted the speaker. He was obviously standing outside. "I'm happy to talk to you, too."

"Kind of busy here, man. What is it, Boone?"

"You need to get your ass back here. And bring Rylee with you."

Shep frowned. "Why? What's going on?"

"I can't say. But make it quick."

Shep's stomach tightened. "What's wrong?"

"Nothing's wrong. But can you pick Rylee up? She mentioned to Sofia that she was going to be home today. Something about cleaning her apartment…"

"I'm actually with her now."

Rylee watched him curiously.

"Perfect," Boone said. "Then head back."

"I don't—"

The line went dead.

Shep took the phone from his ear and stared at it for a second. "What the hell?"

"What's wrong?" Rylee asked.

"He wouldn't say. But he wants us both to come back to the ranch. Like, now."

"Both of us?"

He nodded. She didn't look thrilled. After all, they hadn't ironed out a single thing. Hadn't even had a chance to broach the subject of the other night, let alone fix it.

"I can't imagine what this is all about," he said, "but don't feel like you need to come. This is your Saturday. You probably don't want to spend a chunk of it at the ranch." What he was thinking, but didn't say, was that she probably didn't want to spend a chunk of it with him.

"No," she said. "I'll come. Whatever it is, they want both of us there, so it must be important."

He nodded again. She was being so gracious about the whole thing. But he wasn't surprised. Rylee had always been full of grace.

"We can talk after," he said. "Just you and me, okay?"

"Okay."

They stood there for a minute, silence settling between them. He hated how stilted this was, when for the last few weeks the energy that had flowed between them had been so easy and warm. And now they had to go out to Dalton's Grange and keep pretending...

He felt the muscles in his jaw bunch. It had only been a few days ago that he'd been trying to talk Rylee into marrying him for real. And he felt like she might've been tempted to marry him, too. To actually be his wife, for better or worse. In sickness and health. For *real*. Again, he was struck by how flippant he'd been. How arrogant at thinking a marriage of convenience could happen without strings attached. Major strings.

"Let me get my jacket," Rylee said evenly. "I'll be right back."

He watched her disappear down the hallway.

And wondered again how he could've been so stupid.

Chapter Ten

Rylee sat beside Shep in the cab of his truck, trying to hold back tears. If she weren't so stubborn, she would've let them fill her eyes by now. Maybe they'd even be spilling down her cheeks. But she refused to let him see how hurt she was by all of this. How much this new tension between them broke her heart.

She sneaked a look over at him and wondered again how they'd gotten here. Their night together had been so wonderful, so magical, that she thought he'd have to feel it, too. But there was no rule book that said if one person was in love, the other person had to feel the same. A cruel reminder as she gazed back out the window to watch the businesses and houses in Bronco begin to give way to pastures and lush, green farmland as they made their way toward Dalton's Grange.

Horses and cattle grazed near long stretches of fence line, and the midafternoon sun glinted off the gabled metal roofs of countless barns in the distance. It was beautiful. A gorgeous spring day where the mountains looked more purple than blue, and the snow that graced their peaks reminded Rylee of powdered sugar. A hawk made a lazy circle in the sky above, and she leaned her head back against the rest, taking comfort in the warmth of the sunshine through the window.

Shep reached out and turned on the radio. Probably to fill the empty silence, another arrow to her heart. But there was no use denying it. Things between them were different now. So different that she wondered how they'd ever be able to continue this charade when they got out to the ranch. Everyone would probably know there was something wrong. And then what?

She sighed. She guessed that could be their way out of this lie. They could break up for real (or for fake, she couldn't keep track anymore), and it would all be said and done.

Shep slowed at the long, paved road that led out to the ranch and turned on his blinker. Rylee's stomach dipped at the thought of seeing his parents again. At what their reasoning was for wanting her to come out on a Saturday afternoon. It probably had something to do with the wedding, but what? Maybe they wanted more details or something. Especially if Deborah and Neal thought there was any possibility it would be held at Dalton's Grange. They'd need to start planning. Like, *now*.

Shep cleared his throat. "I'm really sorry about this..."

"Don't be sorry."

Although, the odds were pretty good he wasn't talking about this afternoon. He could be talking about the whole thing, and the thought of that just made her sad. She'd let herself be carried away by this. She'd let herself believe that someone like Shep would truly want to marry someone like her, when they'd always been so different. It wasn't that she didn't think she was good enough for him; it wasn't that. She was confident in the person she was, in the woman she'd become, even though she had to remind herself sometimes. (As a kid, even reminders hadn't done the trick.) But at the same time, she'd always known she wasn't his type. That she lacked the wildness that was so ingrained in his personality. In his very *being*. Even though she was happy with her own personality, she couldn't help but feel like she watered his down some, and that wasn't a good feeling.

The truck made its way down the drive, and the house finally came into view. When it did, Rylee's heartbeat slowed in her chest, and she sat forward to gape at the driveway.

"Uh, Shep?"

He was staring, too. "Oh crap."

The entire drive was full of cars. There must've been twenty of them, and the ones that didn't fit in the big, circular driveway were parked in rows next to the fence line of the south pasture. It looked like a party. A major party.

Rylee's mouth hung open. "What in the world?"

"I should've known this was what they were up to." He rubbed his jaw. "I should've known."

She looked over at him, dread settling like a lead weight in her stomach. "You should've known they were up to *what*?"

But she already knew. It looked like a party because it *was* a party. Probably an engagement party for the two of them. *Oh Lord.* Everyone would be here. All their friends and family. Deborah would've insisted on that part. It would be a big deal, and they would be expected to look happy and in love and very pleasantly surprised.

Rylee had the surprised part down, and even the in-love part. But the happy part? That would be harder to pull off. She felt so unsettled that, again, she had to hold back tears.

Shep pulled the truck over to the side of the drive, behind an expensive-looking Audi, and turned the engine off. The cab was quiet, the sun shining through the windows not nearly as comforting as before. She could feel him watching her. She knew he felt awful about this, and it wasn't his fault. Well, the party wasn't his fault. The other stuff kind of was.

"You don't have to do this, Rylee," he said, his voice gravelly. "I can take you home and make up some kind of excuse. This was a surprise. For all they know, you had something else going on."

"No, Sofia asked a bunch of questions the other night at dinner. She asked if I was going to be home this weekend, things like that. I told her I was doing some spring-cleaning on my apartment today, so they knew I was basically free."

"Yeah, Boone mentioned that. But it still doesn't matter. You can pretend to be sick or something. Anything."

She looked down at her clothes. A T-shirt and jeans. She hoped people wouldn't be dressed up. She didn't look *terrible*, but still. She was completely unprepared. Which, she guessed, was the whole point of a surprise party.

"No," she said. "They went to all this trouble. The least we can do is show up."

He nodded. But it looked like he wanted to say something more. They sat there in silence, sitting so close to each other, but to Rylee, it felt like they were a million miles apart.

"We still need to talk," Shep said.

"Yes."

"When this thing is over…"

"Yes."

He watched her, and she felt the weight of his gaze on her shoulders. When they talked, what would he say? That this had been a mistake from the beginning? That it wasn't her, it was him? Or would it be something else altogether?

She swallowed down the achiness in her throat and unbuckled her seat belt.

"We'd better get in there," she said. "Before they send a search party out."

They got out of his truck. And then they were walking side by side up to the ranch house.

Shep reached over and took her hand. He squeezed it, reassuring her, and she took comfort in his warmth.

The only problem was she had no idea if this was real or all for show.

Shep glanced over at Rylee, his hand on the doorknob. She didn't look back. Just stood there, looking calm and very beautiful and resigned to the fact that they were going to have to face whatever was on the other side of this door as a couple. As an engaged couple.

He didn't think he'd ever loved her more, and that was making him nervous. In fact, it was almost making him break a sweat, and he gritted his teeth, trying for a semblance of the vibe she was putting out. *Relaxed. In control. Able to handle anything.*

"Ready?" he asked.

She nodded. "Ready as I'll ever be."

"Is it bad form to get smashed at your engagement party? Asking for...me."

At that, she did look over. Her lips tilted slightly, her eyes twinkling. So, maybe she didn't hate him as much as he thought she probably did. He hoped not. He knew he was doing a pretty terrible job of redeeming himself for going radio silent over these last few days, but once they got this party out of the way, they could sit down and talk. Properly talk. And maybe he'd be able to articulate what he was feeling. Maybe he'd even have the courage to tell her he loved her. But it needed to happen without all this wedding stuff between them. It needed to be just him and her, and he needed to be able to think about what he was actually going to say. Because it had to be real. All this other stuff was like a circus act—a high wire that they'd been trying to walk for the last few weeks. And he hadn't known until right this minute how precarious that had made them. They could lose everything, their friendship, their entire relationship, with one wrong step.

"I can't wait for a glass of wine," she said. "Or two."

"Same. I was just thinking about a beer. Or a shot of whiskey. Or both."

She smiled, and for the first time since seeing her that day, it didn't look forced. "I'm not quite sure how we let things get to this point," she said. "It all seemed so abstract at the time. A little like a fantasy, I guess. But this is about as real as it gets."

"Amen to that, sister."

She licked her lips. "Shep… I don't know if you're still wanting to get married after what happened the other night. But I wanted to tell you… I wanted to tell you that—"

But before she could finish her sentence, the front door swung open. He and Rylee looked up to see his dad standing there, smiling wide. And behind him, Rylee's parents, Lionel looking a little stiff in a pair of Wranglers and a collared shirt.

God, he thought. *Here we go*.

"Surprise!" everyone yelled in unison. And then from somewhere inside the house, music started playing. Country music with an upbeat tempo. Shep could smell barbecue wafting through the house, probably from the grill out back.

"We thought you two were going to stand out here all day," his dad said, taking his arm and pulling him inside. "Come in here and join your party!"

Shep was vaguely aware of someone shoving a cold beer in his hand, and Rylee being ushered in behind him. All of a sudden, she was swarmed by women. His sisters-in-law, his mother, her mother, Gabby… He caught Rylee's best friend's gaze, and he thought it looked a little chilly. She probably knew about the last few days and was judging him. Rightfully so.

Shep rubbed his throbbing temple.

Someone slapped his back, and he turned to see his cousin Anderson standing there.

"Congratulations, man," Anderson said. "You're finally tying the knot. I didn't think we'd live to see the day, but here it is."

Shep gave him a hug. He and Anderson had always been close. "Thanks for coming, buddy."

"Are you kidding? Marina and I are stoked for you, Shep. Honestly. It seems like so many of our friends are getting divorced lately. We were just talking about it on the way over. It's just nice to see some happiness for a change."

Shep had been so flippant about this in the beginning. He remembered thinking that if it didn't work out with Rylee, they'd just get a divorce. Simple as that. Divorce was obviously necessary for a lot of couples; sometimes marriages just didn't work, and there was no shame in that. But he also knew you shouldn't go into one thinking about divorce first thing. Speaking of flippant...

His neck heated, and his shirt felt itchy, like there might be some bits of hay down his back.

"Yeah," he said, looking over at where Rylee was standing with his mother and Gabby. "I hear you."

"Now, just don't screw it up," Anderson said with a wink. It was meant to be light and teasing. But it hit home like a baseball bat to Shep's chest.

He nodded, managing a smile back. But he felt his teeth grind together, his shoulders tighten. Screwing things up had always been his worst fear. Letting down the people closest to him. Messing things up by getting too invested in them. Was that what he was going to do with Rylee? Was he going to ruin this before it even had a chance to go somewhere? How could he be honest with her, and tell her that he was in love with her, when doing that would mean actually having something to lose? Something significant? The answer was he wasn't sure he could.

He looked over at her again, and this time, she glanced back. She was so gorgeous, so poised. He remembered the little girl who rode her bike with him in the summertime, her copper pigtails flying. And the teenager who swam with him in the river, her skin pale and her body so willowy it seemed like she might blow away in a stiff wind. She'd grown so much since then, but she was also the same in the best ways. She was still the same Rylee... Smart, compassionate, well-read, loving, funny... The list went on and on. Completely different from the women he'd dated in the past.

He watched her, swallowing hard. Rylee was the real deal. The one you brought home to your parents. The one you married, had kids with, had a life with. And then got old with. The one whose hand you held at the very end, when it was all said and done, and you were ready to say goodbye. She was the one.

So why was admitting that so hard? He knew why. It was hard because this wasn't a foregone conclusion for her. And if that was the case, where did that leave him? In love and as unsure of himself as that boy on the bike, that was where.

He rubbed the back of his neck as Anderson told him something about his son Jake's soccer season. He was only half listening. What he really wanted to do was get in his truck, roll down the windows and go for a drive. He needed to think. And being around all these people, as much as he loved them, wasn't helping his mood any.

From somewhere across the living room, someone tapped a fork on a champagne glass. He looked over to see his dad holding said glass in the air.

"Folks!" he said, his voice booming. "I'd like to make a toast."

A hush fell over the room. Shep glanced over at Rylee again. She didn't look thrilled. In fact, she looked like she might want to run away just as much as he did.

"This engagement came as a bit of a surprise," his dad continued, "but we honestly couldn't be happier. We've known the Parkers for a long time. Some of you know that we were neighbors in Tenacity. And, well, Rylee grew up with Shep. Deborah thinks it was meant to be."

A collective *aww* moved through the crowd, and Shep's mother smiled wide. He didn't think she'd ever looked happier. She wanted this so much. He knew her heart attack had something to do with that, and the fact that she'd faced her own mortality on the highest level. She wanted her family happy, all her boys settled. It was important to her.

Shep's stomach dropped into his boots. How would she feel if this marriage immediately ended in an annulment? Or worse, a divorce? What would that do to her?

"Son, I know this party was a surprise," his dad said. "But we knew you and Rylee wouldn't have wanted a big fuss, so this was the only way your mother could work it out. We actually scaled it way down, if you can believe that."

Collective laughter.

"So, a toast…"

Everyone who had a champagne glass or a mug of beer or a glass of soda raised them in the air. Shep had to admit, the whole thing was pretty festive. If it weren't his own engagement party, and if he weren't so upside-down about the whole thing, he'd probably be having a great time.

"To Shep and Rylee," his father said. "We love you both."

The entire room erupted in cheers, and Shep took a long drink of his beer. It warmed his throat on the way down. Rylee was immediately enveloped in hugs, and he could barely catch a glimpse of her from across the room anymore.

"Wait, wait, wait…" This from Holt, who was standing next to the rest of his brothers. His voice was also deep and booming—apparently a Dalton trait. "We want to know when the big day is. Especially if it's gonna be at the ranch. We'll have to clean the place up, put a dance floor in the barn, tell the horses to hit the road…"

More laughter. But the question made Shep's ears burn. *The big day…* Such a simple question for anyone actually getting married. Of course people were expecting to know. He and Rylee were newly engaged, but they'd had plenty of time to narrow it down. Come up with a wedding month at least.

A few weeks ago, Shep wouldn't have had any problem lying about this. He would've simply put it in the "harmless" category, along with everything else. But today, he couldn't seem to open his mouth to utter a single word.

He looked over at Rylee as the room settled down again. As people waited for a response to a seemingly simple question. She was watching him back.

He shifted on his feet, his face growing uncomfortably hot. They were all waiting for him to say something. Anything. Rylee was waiting, too, and he knew what she was waiting for was much more meaningful. She was waiting to see how he'd react to this. To all of it. And all of a sudden, the entire world seemed to be holding its breath as Shep struggled to get a damn clue.

"Cat got your tongue, little brother?"

More laughter. But this time, it was clearly awkward. The moment felt strained. And still, he couldn't seem to get his mouth to cooperate. It was embarrassing. Where were the fun little fibs he and Rylee had been telling for the last few weeks? Where was his characteristic cockiness? It wasn't just that he hadn't answered Holt yet, it was also how he probably looked standing there that was making all his friends and family stare at him now. He felt like a deer in the headlights. And he was sure he looked worse. Much worse.

"Rylee?" Holt said. "Help us out here, since your fiancé seems to have lost all ability to speak. Have you two set a date or what?"

All the curious gazes in the room shifted to Rylee then. Shep's gaze shifted to her, too. As if she might hold the answer to all the questions in his heart. As if what she might say (or not say) would determine the course of the rest of his life.

He watched her, his heart thumping inside his chest. The blood rushing hotly in his ears. The fear that had washed over him the morning after sleeping with her was almost tenfold now. It was carrying him away with all the power of a swollen, rushing river. Intuitively, he felt like he was about to lose her after all.

Her eyes grew glassy. Her chin started trembling. She was obviously trying not to cry.

Enough. He needed to say something to avert whatever was happening here. It didn't matter if it was the truth or another lie, he just needed to protect her the best way he could. Better late than never...

He took a breath, but before he could say anything, she held up her hand. It was for his benefit, he could tell. She probably knew exactly what he'd been thinking just now.

"I'm sorry, everyone," she said. "I know you took time out of your day to come here. And Neal and Deborah, I'm especially sorry to let you both down..."

Shep's mother's expression fell. The tension in the room was now palpable, and Shep felt mildly sick to his stomach.

"But we're not getting married," Rylee said, her voice trembling.

There was an audible gasp. And then Rylee pushed her way through the crowd and was out the front door before Shep could even comprehend what just happened.

Her mother followed her out in a rush, and then the door closed again, leaving everyone standing there quiet and stunned.

Shep could feel their gazes on him. He was numb all over, his stomach turning.

"I'm sorry," he said. Then found there was simply nothing else to say.

He pushed his way through his friends and family, and opened the front door to a blast of cool, spring air. Rylee was standing with her mother on the porch, crying. Her eyes were red and puffy, her face wet with tears.

She looked up at him, but shook her head. "No, Shep."

"Rylee…"

"Mom, can you please take me home?"

Norma frowned, wrapping an arm around her daughter's shoulders. They both walked past him without another word. Heading down the front porch steps to the sea of cars in the driveway.

Shep watched them go, feeling so confused that his throat ached. He hadn't cried since middle school. Not even when his mother had been in the hospital after her heart attack. He was used to keeping his feelings inside, underneath the surface, where nobody could see them and where even he couldn't be bothered by them very often.

But right then, he felt about as raw and vulnerable as he ever had, and he knew as he watched Rylee climb into her parents' Suburban that this was a turning point in his adult life. He had two choices…

Go after her.

Or let her go and let this crazy idea of a marriage, which had little to no chance of actually working—no matter how much he might want it to—go with her.

Chapter Eleven

Rylee sat beside her mom, watching the farmland pass by in a blur. Her eyes had been full of tears ever since they'd driven away from Dalton's Grange, and she kept having to brush them away to be able to see at all.

Her mother looked over at her now. Rylee knew she was worried. But to her credit, she hadn't said anything—she'd just held Rylee's hand, probably sensing that she needed a good cry before she could say anything at all.

Finally, Rylee took a deep breath and wiped the last of her tears away. She didn't think she'd ever experienced this kind of feeling before. Her heart wasn't just broken. It was shattered. And the shards were like thousands of needles inside of her, piercing her consciousness, reminding her with every second that she'd let herself fall in love and hope for something that just wasn't meant to be.

"Are you ready to tell me what's going on?" her mother asked softly. "What happened back there?"

Rylee clasped her hands in her lap, wondering how much she should say. She didn't really think there was any point in telling her the engagement had been fake. It would be hard for her mom to understand, and even harder for Rylee to explain. Her heartbreak was real, and that was all that mattered right now. All her mom needed to know. The rest was history, anyway.

"He wasn't ready," she said. It was the truth. He wasn't ready. Apparently, he just didn't know it until they'd slept together. That was the most painful part.

"Oh, honey…"

"It's okay, Mom. I'll be okay."

"I know you will. You're strong—you've always been strong. But this is a lot."

There was silence for a minute, her mother staring at the road ahead. Rylee picked at a hangnail on her thumb until it started to sting. The windows were cracked, and the fresh air felt good against her feverish cheeks.

"Can I just ask…" her mother finally said. "Why? What happened? I mean, you said he seemed so excited to get married. What changed his mind?"

Rylee didn't know the exact answer to that, but she could guess well enough. Maybe he didn't feel the same about her as she felt about him. That seemed like a logical explanation. Or maybe the thought of marriage in general, to her or anyone else, was starting to be a little too real for comfort. That was also a logical explanation. Or maybe it was a combination of the two. Who knew?

It didn't matter though. She'd been able to see every-thing she needed to see in the living room of his parents' house a half hour ago. The look on his face, his body language when Holt had asked when the wedding would be. And then he simply hadn't been able to open his mouth to answer at all. He'd looked shell-shocked and frozen in place, obviously struggling with the question, when he'd been able to lie about all of this so easily before. It had been one of the most humiliating and hurtful moments of Rylee's life. She hadn't been able to get out the door fast enough.

"I'm not sure," she finally managed. "Things have been different between us this last week, and I knew something was wrong. He's been distant…"

Her mother frowned. Her hair blew in front of her face, and she pushed it away again. "Your father and I were worried this was all happening too fast," she said. "I didn't want to say anything because you don't need our permission, or even our blessing, to live your life the way you want."

"But I did want your blessing."

"I know, and you know we love Shep. But he's always been like this. A risk-taker, when you've always been so careful."

Rylee looked over and gave her a small smile. "Except when I was hanging out with him."

"Yes, exactly that. He used to be able to get you to do things I don't think you normally would have. He had a way of leading you into trouble, and your dad and I were worried this engagement might be history repeating itself. I mean, you barely know each other now. You only reconnected recently."

"I know." It was true. All of it. But still, Rylee felt herself growing defensive of Shep, despite everything. His wildness was what she loved about him. And he hadn't led her into this engagement. She'd gone willingly enough. She'd known the risks, the risks that went along with being with a man like Shep, and she'd accepted them happily. Because it meant being with Shep, and that was all that mattered.

Except now her heart was broken, and those risks

seemed a lot more glaringly obvious in hindsight. How could she have ignored her instincts so easily? How could she have been so naive?

"I'm sorry about this, Mom," she said. "I shouldn't have rushed into it."

"You don't have to be sorry. But, honey…do you love him?" Her mother looked over at her then, her eyes unmistakably sad. "Because if you still love him, and you two talk it out…"

Rylee shook her head. She couldn't, she *wouldn't* let herself hope for more from Shep. He'd made it very clear over the last few days how he felt. And if she had trouble getting the message before, she'd gotten it today. No, talking wouldn't make a difference. Sometimes actions spoke louder than words. She'd seen a glimpse of his fear and doubt today, and she wouldn't let herself be on the receiving end of that any longer than she already had.

"There's really nothing else to say," she said. "He's not ready, but it goes deeper than that. Sometimes love isn't enough. We're just too different, and it kills me to say that, but we are."

Her mother nodded slowly. It made sense.

The only problem was, Rylee didn't quite believe it.

Shep rode alongside his dad, their horses plodding along in unison. The sun was unusually warm this afternoon, and he took his Stetson off to feel the breeze in his damp hair and wipe the sweat from his brow.

His dad had asked him to come along to check the fences, which usually took a few hours. But they'd only been out for about twenty minutes before Shep realized the fences weren't the real reason they were out here. This was his dad's way of initiating a conversation with him about Rylee. He'd bet money on it. And now, all he wanted to do was turn his little chestnut mare around and urge her into a gallop back to the barn. Conversation be damned.

Instead, he put his Stetson back on again, pulling it low over his eyes, and leaned forward in the saddle. Alice's ears flicked back and forth as she waited for him to tell her what to do. She could probably feel the tension in his body, his legs stiffer in the saddle than usual. In fact, his shoulders and back felt stiff, too, and he'd had a continuous headache for about three days now. But he wasn't surprised. He hadn't slept well, had barely eaten since the engagement party from hell. All he could think about was Rylee. Her name throbbed in his mind, like a fever dream that he couldn't shake.

His father leaned on the horn of his saddle. His white gelding, Blanco, lifted his head and tugged on the bit in his mouth, wanting to pick up the pace.

"Whoa, whoa," Neal said in a soothing voice. When he talked to his horses, it was like he was a different man altogether. He was intuitive with animals, exceptionally gentle. When Shep was growing up, he sometimes found himself jealous of them, realizing even at a young age how silly that was, but not being able to help it, either. His father was a tough man in most ways, like most ranchers were, and hadn't left a lot of room for affection for his boys.

Shep understood that better now that he was a man himself. He understood how messy that kind of emotion could be, how much it could complicate everything. At the same time, he couldn't help but feel a little resentful about how that lack of affection was embedded in his very essence. Maybe if he'd learned as a kid to be more in touch with his emotions, and less afraid of them, he wouldn't be in this mess now.

"Son," his dad said, "I haven't wanted to push, but I'm worried about you."

Shep nodded, keeping his eyes on the fence line ahead. "I know you are. But I'm okay."

They were quiet for a minute. Shep knew this kind of talk didn't come naturally to his father. He had to work at it, and Shep wasn't making it any easier by not opening up. But honestly, thinking about Rylee constantly was hard enough. Talking about her was damn near impossible.

"Do you want to tell me what happened?" his dad asked, his saddle creaking underneath him as Blanco stepped over a small log in their path.

"Dad..."

"I know you probably don't want to go over the details, and that's okay. I'm not asking you to. I just want to know what's going on. You seemed so happy before. And now..."

What was he supposed to say to that? It was true. He was miserable. The second Rylee had left Dalton's Grange that day, he'd become a shell of his former self. Trying, without much luck, to get back to how he'd been before he'd run into her at Janet's party. Because it was looking like they'd parted ways now for good. She wasn't answering his calls, and he'd finally just decided to give her space. If that's what she needed, that's what he'd give her.

He took a deep breath, taking in the smell of the grass and of the horse underneath him. Even though the temperature was well over average for spring in Montana, there were angry-looking clouds in the distance. The smell of rain on the breeze promised a storm soon.

"You're right," he said, trying his best to keep his voice even. "I was happy."

"Then what happened?"

Shep shrugged, guiding Alice around another fallen log. He wasn't sure how much he should say. Or how much his dad expected him to say. Heart-to-hearts weren't exactly their style. Still, it felt good knowing this engagement to Rylee wasn't just a footnote in his dad's life. He obviously cared, even though it was hard for him to come right out and say it. He and his youngest son were so much alike, it was scary. And that wasn't a comforting thought. Neal Dalton had changed for the better over the years. But there was no denying the man he used to be.

Shep had the same blood flowing through his veins. Did that mean he was going to make the same idiotic mistakes as his dad? It was the question he'd been asking himself since spending the night with Rylee. The question that had been haunting him since he'd seen her last, driving away in the passenger seat of her parents' SUV. He'd been so tempted to go after her that day. But he'd talked himself out of it because he'd convinced himself that staying away was for her own good. He'd wanted to protect her, to keep her from any pain that he might inflict without even trying.

Shep glanced over at his dad and frowned. He looked tired. Weary. Which wasn't like him. It was enough to make Shep pull lightly on Alice's reins and bring her to a stop.

"What is it, Dad?" he asked.

His father pulled Blanco to a stop, too, and the horses stood side by side, sniffing each other's noses.

The older man sat there and looked out over the pasture to the mountains in the distance. The muscles in his gray, stubbly jaw bunched and then relaxed again. His shoulders were slumped a little, making him look older than he actually was. For a rare moment, Shep was overcome with emotion for his dad. They'd always had a complicated relationship and had sometimes gone for weeks without speaking. But they loved each other. That had never been a problem.

"I know I've made some mistakes with you, son," his father said, his voice gravelly.

"Dad…"

"I have. We both know it. The way I raised you…well, it's probably why you're having such a hard time talking to me now. You're not exactly an open book, Shep."

No, he never had been. So he just sat there, shifting his gaze to the mountains, too. Wishing that relationships, that love of all kinds, didn't have to be so hard.

"Your mother was always the better parent," his dad continued. "She was the nurturer. The one you boys came to when you'd get hurt or into a fight. She picked up the slack when I wasn't around. Physically and emotionally. I know I failed you in a lot of ways."

Shep lowered his head, watching the breeze move through Alice's rust-colored mane. Watching her fuzzy ears flick back and forth. He felt her breathing underneath him, felt her skin twitching at the flies. Everything seemed magnified right then—the sound of the birds in the trees and the insects in the grass. It felt dreamlike, sitting here talking to his father about the past. Something that Neal Dalton didn't love bringing up. He was ashamed of the things he'd done, and preferred keeping them firmly behind him.

But now, sitting here on the back of his favorite horse, it seemed like he was having a moment. For whatever reason, he could see himself in Shep's circumstance. Or, at least, he could see his shortcomings in Shep's shortcomings, which might've been deeper than he'd ever looked before. Shep didn't know if that made him feel better or worse.

"What I'm trying to say," his dad went on, "is that I'm sorry for a lot of things that happened in your childhood. And I'm not sure what I would've done without your mother. She was the glue that held our family together for a lot of years."

Shep nodded. He could remember days when it felt like they were a single-parent family. It hadn't been easy. Even after they'd won the money. And then his mother had her heart attack, and everything had changed. They'd moved from Tenacity, bought Dalton's Grange, and it was like the sun had come out after a long, dark storm. His dad woke up from whatever stupor he'd been in and had started paying attention to his wife and family. In a lot of ways, it was like he was a different person, whom Shep was still getting to know to this day.

He sensed how close his dad's feelings were to the surface now. This kind of display was so unusual that he was afraid to say anything back, for fear of breaking the spell. It was nice hearing him say things like this. It was nice hearing him acknowledge how wonderful his wife was and how grateful he was to her for the years she stuck with him, when quite frankly, not many women would have.

They sat there for a minute, quiet. The horses shaking their heads every now and then and jingling their bridles.

Then, Shep's dad turned in his saddle and pushed his cowboy hat up on his forehead.

"If you love Rylee," he said. "If you truly love her, you should try and make it work."

Shep considered this. He did love her. He knew that now. There was something that happened to you when you were faced with losing someone that made everything else come into sharp focus. It was probably the exact same thing that had happened to his dad.

The problem was Shep didn't know how to navigate it. How was he supposed to love her the way he wanted to love her and not be terrified of losing that feeling someday? Or worse, losing her? It went against every single instinct he had to protect himself. It was an awful feeling to be so sure about something, yet so unsure of it at the same time.

"I love her," he said. "But I'm not sure she wants it to work."

"Are you positive about that?"

"I'm not positive about anything. Except how amazing she is. I'm not quite sure what she sees in me."

"Shep," his father said, his voice suddenly sharp. "Don't be stupid."

Shep raised his eyebrows.

"You heard me. You're a good man, and I think it's pretty obvious that she loves you. But I can understand the doubt. Hell, I doubt myself all the time. I'm a flawed person. But I decided I'm not going to live my life in fear of what might or might not happen. Especially with things that are out of my control. The only thing you can do, Shep, is try to be a good human. A loving person. To appreciate your friends and family, and the rest is going to be out of your hands. The sooner you accept that, the sooner you can stop running away from your life and get down to living it."

Shep sat there in stunned silence. It was maybe the most advice he'd ever gotten from his father. Ever. It was absolutely the most heartfelt thing he'd said in a long time. And it made absolute sense. Was that what was happening here? Was Shep running away from life?

He looked out over the pasture as Alice shifted restlessly underneath him. He'd never thought of himself as fearful. In fact, he'd always thought of himself as exactly the opposite. Strong, independent, a bold streak a mile long. But the truth was, when it came to women, he'd never let himself get close enough to risk a damn thing. And wasn't that the definition of fear itself?

"I don't want to lose her," he said quietly.

His dad nodded, then pulled his hat low over his eyes. "I know you don't." And then, without another word, he nudged Blanco forward. The horse obliged with a soft nicker.

Shep sat there watching them go, thinking of what had just happened between him and his father. Thinking about what had happened between him and Rylee over these last few weeks, and how much it had changed him. He hadn't realized it until right that minute, but it had. *She'd* changed him. The question now was, was it too late to convince her of that?

With a squeeze of his legs, he nudged Alice forward, too.

Rylee reached out and rubbed a clear spot in the foggy windshield. The wipers were going as fast as they could, but her car was having trouble keeping up with the sudden nasty weather.

Leaning back again, she looked over at the small box in her passenger seat. The pearl necklace that she was just now getting around to returning to Mayor Smith and his poor wife. She was embarrassed it had taken this long to bring it back. But to be fair, her mind had been kind of occupied with other things lately.

At the thought of the necklace, her stomach dropped. It was impossible not to linger on the memory of Shep teasing her about wanting to see her wearing it and nothing else the night they'd slept together. She'd been so happy in his arms that night. Almost euphoric. And then it had all come crashing down.

She looked back at the road, feeling an ache rise in her throat. She swallowed it back down with a new, welcome stubbornness. Any time she felt like dissolving into tears over Shep, she simply refused to give in. She couldn't thank any particular strength for that; she was just tired of crying. It was getting her nothing but swollen eyes and a chapped nose, and she was desperate to move on from him and this whole ridiculous engagement.

The problem was, though, she couldn't.

Trying to ignore the painful squeeze of her heart, she peered through the frantic windshield wipers to the street beyond, looking for the mayor's address. It'd be dark pretty soon, and then she'd have an even harder time seeing where she was going through this downpour. Not the best time to be driving to Tenacity after this, but she was long overdue for a vacation, and her parents had been wanting her to come home for a while now. Truthfully though, the timing was perfect, since the thought of staying in Bronco a second longer was too much to bear. She needed to get her head on straight again, and she was hopeful that might happen a little faster in a familiar setting, with the comfort of her mom nearby.

She squinted through the dusky evening light, seeing the mayor's house finally come into view. It was big and fancy, and wasn't very distinguishable from the other big, fancy houses on the street. But the address was right there, in bold black numbers on the garage.

She eased up to the curb and cut the engine. Then sat there for a minute with the rain drumming on the roof. She felt blue from the miserable weather and lonesome beyond belief. She missed Shep so much that sometimes she didn't think she'd be able to stand it one second longer.

Lifting her chin, she forced a deep, even breath. It was true that she hadn't answered the handful of times he'd called. But he hadn't shown up in person, either, and that was what really needed to happen for any of this to get sorted through. But, she reminded herself again, there wasn't really anything to sort through, was there? After she'd left Dalton's Grange the day of the party, it had taken a while for everything to sink in. But when it had, she realized how truly crazy this whole thing had been from the beginning. She'd let herself fall in love with an idea. A romantic notion that their promise had actually meant something. When in reality, the promise they'd made the day she'd left for college had simply been a way for her and Shep to make their goodbye easier. Lighter. More bearable. And she'd wanted so badly to believe it had been real that she'd let herself fall back in love with him.

She stared through the rain streaming down the windshield. She simply hadn't realized how easy it would be to love Shep again. She'd let her guard down. But then again, she hadn't thought she would need to protect herself from him. She hadn't thought he'd hurt her like this. Which was stupid. Looking back, she should've known he wouldn't be able to commit. Even to a pretend engagement or marriage. Shep wasn't the settling-down type, never had been, and she'd *known* that. So she guessed a good portion of this was on her. Plain and simple.

She reached over and tucked the small box into the inside pocket of her jacket, then opened the door into the rain. It immediately hit her in the face—big, cold drops that chilled her to the bone. She needed to remember to keep an umbrella in her car. She never thought of it until it was actually raining, which made her want to groan.

Holding her jacket collar snug around her neck, she ran up the walkway to the front door. When she got there, she shook out her hair and rang the doorbell. She probably looked like something out of *Night of the Living Dead*, but she knew the mayor would be so happy to have the necklace back, he wouldn't care.

After a few seconds, the door opened and Mayor Rafferty Smith stood there looking at her curiously, a glass of what appeared to be bourbon in his hand.

"Hi, Mayor," Rylee said. "I'm Rylee Parker. I met you a few months ago at the convention center. I'm the director of marketing—I'm not sure if you remember. Chuck Carter gave me your address…"

His bushy eyebrows shot up. "Rylee! Of course. What are you doing out in this weather? Come in, come in."

Rylee stepped inside and was immediately met with the smell of woodsmoke. A cozy fire was crackling in the fireplace, and soft lighting glowed throughout the living room. The rain tapped on the windows outside, and all of a sudden, she felt so tired she thought she could curl up on the overstuffed sofa and fall asleep right then and there.

"Please, sit," the mayor said. "My wife is playing Bunco with friends tonight, or she'd make you some of her famous peppermint hot chocolate. It's a perfect night for it."

Rylee sat on the sofa, grateful for the pulsing warmth of the fire. She hadn't realized she was shaking until right that minute.

"Thank you so much," she said. "But I can't stay long. I'm heading to Tenacity after this, and I think it's only going to start raining harder. I want to get a jump on it."

"Oh?" The mayor sat opposite her, the ice tinkling in his glass. "What's in Tenacity, if you don't mind me asking?"

"My family. I try and get back when I can, but work keeps me pretty busy."

"I can imagine." He smiled, obviously curious as to why she was there, but doing his best not to show it. Rylee had always liked him. He seemed like a nice man.

"I'm sorry to just appear on your doorstep like this, Mayor, but—"

"Rafferty, please."

"Rafferty. But I have something for you. I think you'll be happy to have it back." She pulled the box out of the pocket of her jacket and handed it over. "It's a long story, but I think this belongs to you. Or to your wife."

"Is this what I think it is?"

Rylee watched him open the box and pull out the pearl necklace with a gasp.

Looking up at her, he shook his head. "Where did you

find it? I didn't think we'd ever get it back. We'd just about given up hope."

"I went to a birthday party a few weeks ago and saw a friend there." She swallowed hard. The fact that she was now calling Shep just a friend sent brand-new shock waves through her heart. "He'd seen this necklace at a vintage shop and bought it for our other friend's birthday present. When he described it, I told him it sounded like the necklace you bought your wife for your anniversary."

"Thirty years…" the mayor said.

"Yes. A really special anniversary, and a special anniversary gift."

"So, it ended up at a vintage shop, huh?"

"It did."

"And then it ended up at this birthday party."

Rylee nodded.

"And now it made it all the way back to us, thanks to you."

"I'm just sorry I didn't bring it back sooner. I've been…" Her voice suddenly hitched in her throat, and she found that she couldn't finish her sentence. She looked down at her hands in her lap, unable to hold the mayor's gaze anymore for fear she might start crying. And that would just be mortifying.

He leaned forward, putting his elbows on his knees. "You've been what?"

The rain continued tapping on the windows outside. Insistent, chilly. But it was so cozy and welcoming in this living room, and she felt such genuine warmth coming from the man across from her that she looked up and answered honestly.

"I've been distracted. I'm going through a breakup."

He frowned. The firelight flickered across his weathered features, and he nodded knowingly. "Oh, I've been there. Well, not for over thirty years, obviously. But I'm sorry. I know how much it hurts."

Rylee wondered if the pain was etched all over her face. Probably. It felt like she was walking around with a neon sign pinned over her heart that said Warning: Handle with Care.

The mayor looked down at the pearl necklace that was still laced through his fingers and squeezed it in his fist. "You'll probably think I'm crazy," he said. "But I'm starting to think this necklace might be a good luck charm."

"Oh?"

"Do you believe in things like that?"

Rylee had carried around a tiny piece of her baby blanket in her wallet for years because her nana had quilted it, and she thought it was good luck. So, yeah. She did believe in things like that.

"I do," she said. "But what makes you think it's good luck?"

He shrugged and took a sip of his bourbon. "I don't know. Just a feeling I have. I mean, for one thing, it managed to find its way back to us, and what are the odds of that? Like finding a needle in a haystack."

She nodded. *And then some...*

"I'm just saying," he continued, "don't be surprised if your own luck changes pretty soon, young lady."

"What do you mean?"

"I mean this breakup might mend itself. You never know." He winked. "Necklace magic."

For the first time since sitting down, Rylee wondered how much he'd had to drink. The necklace having some kind of special power was a fun thought, but not quite something a totally sober adult would adhere to.

She smiled and looked over at the fire. "I'm not sure he's interested at this point."

"Oh, I doubt that. Sometimes it just takes a man a while to realize what he's got. And then a light bulb goes off. At least, that's what happened with me and my wife."

Rylee glanced back at him.

"And remember," he continued, "thirty years. We've been married a long time, so I know what I'm talking about. She's the love of my life, but I almost walked away in the beginning because I was petrified. And I'm telling you, that's pretty common."

She knew that was true. More than true. In fact, it was like Rafferty Smith had morphed into some kind of bourbon-drinking, super-power-believing relationship guru in the last five minutes, and it was hard not to laugh at the ridiculousness of it all. Her heart felt lighter for the first time in days, and she got up to give him a quick hug.

"Thank you, Mayor," she said.

"Rafferty."

She smiled, pulling away again. "Rafferty. Thank you."

"Thank *you*. For bringing the necklace back. And for reminding me how lucky I am. You just keep your chin up. It'll work out for you, too. I promise."

Rylee looked down at the necklace in his hand. She'd love to believe it had some kind of magic that would rub off on her and Shep. It had brought them back together, after all. But there was so much doubt and fear to get through. She was scared of this. It wasn't just Shep who was struggling. She was struggling, too.

Forcing her gaze away from the lovely string of pearls,

she zipped her jacket up to her chin. She had a long drive in this rain and a lot of thinking to do.

"Have a good evening, Rafferty," she said. "And happy belated anniversary to you and your wife."

He stood and smiled down at her. "You drive safe, now."

Chapter Twelve

Rylee turned the radio down. The rain was coming harder now, and it was so dark that she was having trouble seeing the fog line on the road ahead. She was almost home. Only fifteen minutes away, but it felt like a lifetime with the highway so eerily deserted like this. The clouds and rain were choking out the light of the moon overhead, making her heart beat nervously inside her chest.

Ever since she'd left Bronco, she hadn't been able to stop thinking about Shep. About what it was that had happened between them. Even now, she wasn't exactly sure. Had it been a fling? An actual relationship created from a fake one? Or had it simply been a way for Shep to sow some wild oats, like he was so prone to do?

It hurt to think that maybe it hadn't meant as much to him as it had to her, but at this point, she had to consider the possibility. She had to face the fact once and for all that Shep didn't seem to feel the same about her. He didn't love her. It was a bleak realization and a sad acceptance. Especially after sleeping with him and falling even harder than she ever would've thought possible.

Frowning, Rylee squinted through the darkness and rain. The wind buffeted her little car, and she squeezed the steering wheel with both hands, trying to stay within the lines. If she'd known it would get this bad, she would've waited until morning to leave. But she'd been so ready to get out of Bronco that she hadn't been thinking clearly. She'd only been thinking of Shep and the unrelenting pain in her heart.

The wind gusted again, this time pushing the car toward the middle of the road, where the water was collecting in dark, ominous pools. Rylee felt the tires leave the asphalt in a brief hydroplane before she got control of the wheel again. She glanced over at her phone in the passenger seat, wondering if there was service all the way out here.

And then the car hydroplaned again.

Shep rolled over in bed and opened his eyes to the gritty light of dawn filtering in through the window. The storm last night had pounded the ranch, sending torrents of rain against his bedroom window and keeping him awake until almost three. He'd finally fallen into a restless sleep and had dreamed of Rylee. She'd been trying to call him, and every time he picked up the phone, it went dead, and he couldn't call her back, no matter how many times he tried. It was the kind of dream that left a bad feeling, even long after waking up.

He was so tired now it felt like he was blinking through sandpaper. His muscles were weary and achy. Even his bones didn't seem to want to cooperate inside his limbs, and for the first time in a long time, he felt old.

He was going to be thirty in a few weeks. And thirty was hardly old. But for some reason, Shep felt every single year like a weight strapped to his shoulders. Symbolic and unwavering. Not letting him forget the fact that he was facing this milestone alone. Sure, he had friends and family. But he didn't have the one person who understood him better than anyone else in the world. And that was Rylee. It was all his damn fault that she wasn't waking up beside him now. Curled into his side, her hair fanned out over her pillow in waves of auburn silk. How could he have let her go? The best thing that had ever happened to him, and he'd let her slip right out of his hands.

He pushed himself up on his elbow and stared out the window. The sky had cleared, and he could see the mountains in the distance, cutting a crisp blue line against the grainy dawn sky. He couldn't stop thinking of what his dad had said yesterday. *The sooner you accept that, the sooner you can stop running away from your life and get down to living it.* Those words had echoed in his mind over and over again last night. Until his body had practically hummed with them, until they'd seeped into his subconscious, and he'd fallen asleep with them tapping against his heart, like the chilly spring rain tapping against the window.

Get down to living it...

He lay there now, feeling a strange kind of peace wash over him.

Because he knew what he had to do to get right again.

Shep stood outside Rylee's door and knocked again. This time harder. When he'd gotten in his truck to come into town, he hadn't really considered the possibility that he wouldn't be able to find her. It was anticlimactic. And frustrating as hell.

He raised his hand to knock again, when someone cleared their throat behind him.

He turned to see Gabby standing there, holding the hand of a little girl who couldn't be more than two or three. She smiled up at him. She had chocolate smeared around her mouth.

"She's not home," Gabby said, her voice unmistakably cool.

Shep took his Stetson off and clutched it to his chest. It wasn't like him to feel this uncertain about things. But right now, standing in front of this woman who had nothing but daggers in her eyes for him, he knew he needed to tread lightly. She probably knew where Rylee was, and if he wasn't careful, she'd tell him to go straight to hell.

"Hi, Gabby," he said. He looked down at the adorable little girl who looked so much like her mom. "Who's this?"

"This is Bella. Bella, say hello, honey."

"We came to get Rylee's UFP box," the toddler said, waving with a sticky-looking hand. Shep felt his insides melt. What a cutie. She was almost cute enough to make him forget why he'd come in the first place. Almost.

"The UPS box," her mother corrected gently.

He fixed his gaze on Gabby again and hoped that he looked appropriately pathetic. "I was hoping you could tell me where she is."

Gabby watched him, narrowing her eyes a little. She was obviously weighing whether or not to say anything. But after a moment, some of the stiffness left her shoulders and she sighed.

"You really hurt her, you know."

"I know."

"And I shouldn't tell you sh—" She stopped herself and glanced down at her daughter. "I shouldn't tell you diddly-squat."

Shep smiled. He was making progress. "I know that, too."

"But you look like a man who might be trying to redeem himself, so…"

"I am. I really, really am, Gabby."

She frowned then and grazed her bottom lip with her teeth. "Then I'll tell you…she's fine. She's okay. But she had an accident on the way to her parents' place in Tenacity last night."

Shep's heartbeat slowed, and he felt himself go cold all over. *Accident… Tenacity…* He'd had no idea she was even going back to Tenacity. But then again, why would he? He hadn't come to see her until just now.

"An accident?" he managed. "Is she all right? What happened?"

"Her car went off the road in the rain. She's got some bruises, but other than that, she's fine. She's really lucky."

Shep barely heard that last part. He was already heading down the apartment steps toward his truck.

"Thank you!" He waved over his shoulder.

"Shep," Gabby called after him. "She might not want to see you."

"I know, and that's okay. But I need to tell her something."

Shep climbed in his truck and turned on the engine, revving it without meaning to. He could barely keep his foot off the gas pedal.

Rylee sat on her parents' couch, a fire crackling in the fireplace beside her. Her mother had brought her a quilt and a cup of tea a few minutes ago, and she was having trouble keeping her eyes open.

She took a sip of the tea and winced. Every muscle

in her body was sore. But nothing was broken. Her neck moved back and forth just fine; she could wiggle her fingers and toes, and aside from a small cut on her temple where she'd hit her head against the window, most of her bruises were hidden by clothing. So, all in all, she was doing okay. It could have been so much worse. Her Toyota was probably totaled though, since it was older, so she'd have to figure that out. But her raise at the convention center would cover it. She just hated to say goodbye to that car. She'd had it since her high-school graduation, and she'd taken a lot of road trips in it. She felt like she'd grown up in that car.

She thought about pulling up to Shep's house in it on the day she'd left for California. He'd leaned against the hood, his skin a deep golden brown. His hair had been longer back then, curling around his ears in sandy blond tufts. He'd been so sexy that she remembered having to literally look away for fear he'd be able to tell what she was thinking.

It had been years, but she was finally able to admit how in love she'd been as a teenager. It'd been way more than a schoolgirl crush. For a long time, Shep had been her very best friend. He'd been her family and her confidant. She'd loved him for everything he was, and that included all his faults, which she'd been able to see clearly, even at seventeen. She'd simply cared for him in a way that she'd never cared for anyone before or since, and that made her heart ache even more this morning. Knowing that she'd been so close to being with him, *really* being with him, and it had all crumbled at her feet. The only thing left was dust.

She stared into the fire, its sparking orange flames licking the air. She hoped eventually they'd be able to get past this and be friends again. In some capacity, at least. But some time had to pass first, and she needed perspective to be able to heal. The heartache wasn't going to kill her. At moments, it felt like it might, but it wouldn't. She'd move on, and she'd learn from this. She'd protect herself at all costs, wouldn't love so easily next time and wouldn't give so much of herself so fast. All rules to live by. Rules that she'd discovered a little too late this time around.

From outside, she could hear the faint sound of a vehicle coming up the dirt drive. The neighbor's shepherd mix, Henry, barked in the distance.

Rylee sat up straighter, pain screaming through her core, and listened to the slight rumbling get louder and louder. It wasn't a car coming down their driveway—it was a truck.

She froze, her heartbeat thumping in her ears. It wasn't beyond the realm of possibility that Shep would show up here. Then again, he hadn't shown any interest in seeing her since their engagement party. Even though they'd agreed on talking things out before they'd gotten there. The events of the afternoon had blown that plan right out of the water.

She sat completely still, hating herself for how much she wanted it to be him. Despite everything. And that broke her all over again.

Her mother came into the living room, apparently hearing Henry, too. He was a good watchdog. Almost never wrong. Any time he got to barking, there was a reason to look out the window.

Her mom stood there, the expression on her face drawn. "He's here," she said. "I don't suppose you'll want to talk to him. I can say you're not up to it…"

Rylee let out a breath. So, he'd come to Tenacity. She prayed she had the strength to resist his charms this time. But maybe he just wanted to talk like he had before. And that made perfect sense. They *should* talk. Everything just felt so turned around and upside down, she didn't know if she was even up to that. The only thing she knew for sure was that she didn't want to hurt again like she'd hurt after that party.

"I'll see him, Mom," she said. "It's okay."

Her mother watched her closely for a few seconds. And then, there was the sound of a truck door slamming. Of boots thudding up the porch steps. And then, there was a knock on the screen door.

"Are you sure about this, Rylee?"

She swallowed with some difficulty. Her tongue felt thick and dry in her mouth. "I'm sure." That was a lie. But it was what it was.

Nodding, her mom opened the door. From where she sat on the couch, Rylee could see Shep standing on the porch with his hat in his hand. He wore a blue plaid shirt and worn-out jeans. His dark blond hair bore its characteristic hat ring that always made her heart skip a beat.

"Hi, Mrs. Parker," he said.

"Shep."

"I came to see Rylee. I know she might want to tell me to jump off a cliff, but I was hoping that could be in person."

Her mother gave Rylee a sidelong glance. She wanted to protect her daughter. But at the same time, she knew how she felt about this man. He had the power to make her miserable. Or ridiculously happy. It was a crapshoot.

She turned back to Shep, her stance rigid. "You know she had an accident last night…"

"I do."

"So you can probably guess she's exhausted."

"I won't stay long. I just want to see her. I should've come before this. I wish I had a good reason for staying away, but I don't. At least, not one that you'd probably want to hear right now. But I'd really like to talk to her. And then I'll go back to Bronco, and you won't see me again unless she wants you to. I promise."

Rylee's mother stood there, holding the screen door open a crack and contemplating that. Rylee watched them both, her heart beating in her throat.

"Okay," her mom said after a long minute. "Come on in."

The look of relief on his handsome face was so obvious that Rylee wondered again why he was here. Was this a visit to ease his conscience? Or was he after something else altogether?

She sat up straighter, the pain in her muscles making her want to whimper. But she clamped her lips together as he stepped through the door. His deep blue gaze swept the room and then came to rest on her. She felt it settle there like something warm and comforting and longed for. She'd missed those eyes. That supremely confident look on his face. But he also looked different somehow. There was an expressive, vulnerable tilt to his lips that she'd never seen before. He smiled, but the cockiness was gone. So was the playfulness. In their place was something more serious.

He walked over and leaned down to give her a kiss on the cheek. His stubble scraped her skin in that delicious way that she'd come to love so much.

Setting his hat on the end of the couch, he pulled in an audible breath. "Can I sit?"

"Of course."

She was vaguely aware of her mother leaving the room. Giving them privacy to talk. She heard her bedroom door close from down the hall.

Shep sat beside her, and she could immediately feel the heat radiating from his body. It was almost like the warmth from the fire, only better. She hadn't realized how sad she'd been, how empty she'd felt, until just now. Which made her wary. Without meaning to, she leaned away a little, wanting to stay as aloof as possible, but knowing how futile that probably was.

After a few seconds, she glanced over at him. His eyes were full of concern. He kept looking at the cut on her temple, and she reached up and moved her hair over it.

"I came to your apartment this morning and saw Gabby," he said. "She told me what happened."

Rylee nodded. "I had to talk her out of coming. I'm fine, though. Really."

"You don't look fine."

"It scared me, but I'm okay."

"Well, I'm not okay. I'm not okay by a long damn shot."

She pinched the edge of the blanket between her thumb and forefinger, wishing she at least had some mascara on. Or some lip gloss. Or something.

Shep leaned forward and put his elbows on his knees. Then scrubbed both hands through his hair. She could smell the soap on his skin, the faint scent of hay and leather and man. It made her stomach drop like she was on some kind of roller coaster. And she guessed that was exactly what this was. A Shep Dalton roller coaster, full of twists and turns, ups and downs.

"I don't know what I'd do if something ever happened to you," he said, his voice low. He looked toward the fire, and she could see that he really meant it.

"Shep—"

"No. I need to say some things. And then you can tell me to get out, or whatever you want to tell me. And believe me, I'll understand if that's what it comes to. But I need you to know why I acted the way I did at the party."

All of a sudden, Rylee wasn't sure she wanted to know. Maybe some things were better left unsaid. She and Shep could forget about being lovers and go back to being friends, which was what they'd always been good at. They could chalk these last few weeks up to some kind of adventure gone awry and get back to the comfortable place they'd been their entire young lives. It was possible. Anything was possible.

"Sometimes I wonder if you know how special you are," he said.

She had a strange feeling he must be talking about someone else. Because she'd never thought of herself as anything much to write home about. She knew she was smart, but a lot of people were smart. She was reasonably attractive, but not nearly as pretty as most of Shep's girlfriends were growing up. She was funny enough to be entertaining in a pinch and sensitive enough to cry at sappy commercials, but special? Not really.

But here was this man, this man whom she thought of as nothing *but* special, uttering these words and wanting her to believe them. It was a tall order when you'd spent your whole life thinking of yourself in a certain way.

"You are, you know," he continued. "You always have been. Even when we were little kids, there was something about you that stuck. When you left for school, I missed you so much it was like a part of myself left, too. And when I saw you again at Janet's party..." He shook his head. "It was like that part of me, that puzzle piece, slid right back into place again."

Rylee's heart was beating so fast, it felt like it might pound right through her chest. Shep was describing the exact feeling that she'd had for him back then. And the exact feeling she'd had when she'd seen him at the party. She'd felt like a piece of her had been returned. Like she was complete again after all this time.

And now, here he was. Putting words to those feelings that had been huddling at the deepest, farthest corners of her heart. It took her breath away. But at the same time, she didn't want it to be taking her breath away. She wanted to be stoic. In charge of her emotions. Unable to be swayed by that look in his eyes that was melting away all of her defenses. She thought she'd been prepared for this. But she hadn't been prepared at all.

"I didn't know you felt that way," she said.

"You wouldn't. Because I don't have a great track record of being honest about how I'm feeling."

She gave him a small smile. Truer words had never been spoken.

"It scared me, Rylee," he said. "All of it seemed to happen at once. In the beginning, the engagement seemed harmless and fun. But then it started to mean something. It started to mean everything... And we spent the night together, and before I knew it, I was falling for you."

Rylee's pulse slowed. *Falling for you...* She could

hardly believe what she was hearing. It was too good to be true. And in her experience, any time something seemed too good to be true, it usually was.

He ran his hands down his thighs, like he might be nervous. Shep wasn't the type to get nervous. At least, she'd never known him to be, and she knew him pretty well. But this conversation was blowing everything she thought she knew about him right out of the water.

"But there's one problem with falling for you," he said.

"What's that?"

"You're too good for me."

She stared at him. She'd always thought it was the other way around. He was too good for her. Too handsome, too sexy, too charming. The list went on and on. She'd never really let herself imagine a relationship with Shep because she thought he was out of her league, always had been. Yet here he was, telling her these things. Making her question everything. Definitely making her forget to be wary, and that was a very dangerous thing.

She looked down at her hands in her lap, the quilt a colorful backdrop against her pale skin. She wanted to believe this. She *so* wanted to believe it. But love was a tricky thing. No matter how strong it was, no matter how sweet, it usually came with a healthy dose of fear. At least, that was how it was for her. She thought about what the mayor said last night, about how his own fear had almost derailed his relationship so long ago. And now look at him and his wife—married thirty years. It was a comforting thought.

"Say something," Shep said.

She could feel his gaze on her. Questioning. Heavy. She wasn't sure what he wanted her to say, but so many things were swirling around in her mind right then that she didn't think she could articulate any of them if she tried.

"It's just hard for me," she finally managed. "To believe you'd ever think I was too good for you."

"Why? Why is that so hard to believe?"

She laughed. "Shep. We're *so* different. You were always the popular one. The fun one. The one everyone wanted to be around. I was never like that. I blended. Everywhere I went, I blended in. The only reason I wasn't completely invisible was because I was so close to you. You made people notice me by association."

He watched her, looking incredulous. "Rylee…"

"You have to remember that about me. And I'm okay with it. I'm comfortable in my skin now. I'm happy with who I am. But too good for you? Is that just a line?"

Slapping his thighs, he stood up with a groan. Then walked over to the window and looked out toward the pastures in the distance. Rylee's family's ranch was small. Much smaller than Shep's had been, and nothing in comparison to Dalton's Grange. But it was beautiful land. Some of the prettiest in Tenacity, and she loved it completely. Having Shep standing there, with the ranch stretching in front of him through the single-pane windows, was doing something to her heart.

"You know," he said, turning to her again, "one of the things I love about you is that you don't know how amazing you are. How beautiful you are…"

Her stomach dipped at that. Another drop on the Shep Dalton roller coaster.

"It's the strangest thing. It's like you don't know when other guys look at you. Or when other women are jealous of you. And to me, it's the most obvious thing in the entire damn world." He fixed her with a hard look. "You're the entire package, Rylee, and you don't even know it."

"Shep..."

"And I came here to tell you that I'm falling in love with you."

She blinked up at him. It felt like all the oxygen had been sucked out of the room, and she was breathing through a straw. Her lungs weren't working right. Her throat wasn't working right. He was falling in love with her? Why now?

He frowned and rubbed the back of his neck. "And I'm pretty freaked out right now, Rylee. Because before, when I was pushing to get married, I was only thinking about today. Not about tomorrow, and who doesn't think about tomorrow when they're talking about marriage? It was stupid. I wasn't treating it with the respect it deserves. Or treating you with the respect you deserve."

Swallowing hard, she sat up straighter. Her nose stung, her eyes stung, like she might start crying, and she didn't want to do that. She wanted to be clearheaded for this. This was a conversation that had been a long time coming. Maybe her entire life. She thought of the string of pearls that she'd brought back to the mayor last night and how he'd told her they might be good luck. Was it possible that he'd been right? That a stroke of luck or fate or magic, even, had brought her and Shep back together again? Her heart warmed at the thought.

"I wasn't treating it that way, either, Shep," she said. "There were two people pretending to be engaged, not just one. But I don't regret it because it was maybe the most fun I've ever had. And I've had a lot of fun with you."

He smiled, those two long, irresistible dimples cutting into his cheeks. He looked so young, standing there in the afternoon light, that her throat ached. She wished it could be like this forever. With the two of them on the cusp of something special. With time stretched ahead of them like a long country road. It was scary to think of what could happen if she let herself trust this, if she let herself trust him.

"Why did you do it?" he asked. "Why did you go along with it?"

It was a fair question. And one he probably thought he already knew the answer to. Rylee had gone along with a lot of things he suggested over the years, after all. But this time was different. And she could admit that to herself now. A few weeks ago, it had been hard to admit anything. But now, she could.

She grazed her bottom lip with her teeth, focusing on the feeling. On the taste of her ChapStick on her tongue. She took a deep breath and prayed that when she said what she was about to say, she would be strong enough to walk away from this if it wasn't right for her. Just because you cared about someone deeply didn't always mean you belonged with them. Even if it was Shep she was talking about. They simply might not be right for each other, and at the end of the day, that was okay. It didn't mean she cared for him any less.

"Rylee?" he asked. Waiting. Expectant.

If she'd been standing up right then, her knees might've buckled. She was glad she was sitting down.

"I went along with it," she said quietly, "because I love you. I've always loved you."

He stared down at her. The logs shifted in the fireplace, sending sparks floating into the chimney.

This was the most honest she'd ever been with Shep. It felt strange telling him how she really felt, when she'd spent so long keeping it inside. She never thought she'd tell him this secret. She never thought she'd even admit it out loud, but here she was.

"You've always loved me..." he repeated slowly.

She nodded.

"Since we were kids?"

She nodded again. Thinking of all the time they'd spent together back then, all the adventures they'd gone on. How she felt like she'd follow him anywhere, on any path, no matter how dark and winding. And then, they'd been on the brink of marriage. *Marriage.* She'd been about to follow him into that, too. It was a testament to how much power he had over her. She reminded herself how important it was now not to follow, but to walk side by side.

"You were my best friend, Shep," she said. "You were there for me when I felt the loneliest of my whole life. When I felt awkward and weird and didn't have any other friends. You were always there for me. How could I not love you?"

He listened, letting the words settle. Now he knew. Now there really was nothing left unsaid, and that was a good feeling for her. No matter what ended up happening between them, they were finally being honest with each other.

He walked over and sat down again. This time closer. His thigh brushed against hers, and even through the quilt, there was a familiar electricity there. Her chest tightened with longing. She thought she'd always long for Shep in some form or another. Maybe that part was just meant to be.

"So, you've always loved me," he said quietly. "And I'm falling in love with you. Tumbling head over heels, more like it."

The corners of her lips tilted at that.

"So, now what?" he continued. "What do we do about this, Rylee Parker?"

She took a deep breath. That was a good question. The best question she'd heard in a long time because the possible answers could take them in so many different directions.

"I just know that I want you in my life," she said. "It's more colorful with you in it."

He smiled. He was gorgeous, all tanned and scruffy, his hair messy from his Stetson. He smelled so good that Rylee was having trouble not throwing her arms around him, but she was trying to show some restraint. At least a little bit. She needed some control right now to get through whatever was going to happen next. Because, despite all of this, nothing said they would end up together. That wasn't promised. Nothing was promised.

"I want to show you something," Shep said. "You're probably sore as hell, but I'll carry you there if I have to. Are you up to it?"

She watched him, her heart swelling. When it came to Shep, her heart had trouble not swelling. It was as simple as that.

"I'm up to it," she said.

Chapter Thirteen

Shep walked behind Rylee up the forested path, watching her wince when she stopped to take a breath. He hadn't been kidding when he'd offered to carry her back at the house. And then again when they'd gotten out of the truck. But she'd just laughed and insisted on walking on her own. Probably a good idea. If she'd been in his arms, he would've had trouble not kissing her neck, her cheeks, her lips. It was driving him crazy being this close and not touching her at all. But he wanted to show her the tree first. In order to tell her what he hoped for their future, she needed to understand how he felt about their past.

"Are you sure you're okay?" he asked.

"I'm all right. Just a little sore."

"It's just a few more yards."

She looked up through the canopy of pine trees and smiled. "When you said you wanted to take me to our old stomping grounds, I was thinking more along the lines of the strip mall or the movie theater. Or maybe the river. I haven't been up here in ages."

"I know. Me neither. It's kind of out of the way, and parts of it are being developed. But the trail is the same. And so is the meadow. For now, at least."

"It would break my heart if anyone built on that meadow."

"They might someday. Tenacity isn't as small as it used to be. But at least we'll have the memories."

"And we have a lot of those."

They did. They had so many. Their lives had been so intertwined that sometimes Shep forgot which memories were Rylee's and which were his.

She put her head down and stepped forward on the trail. He followed her, breathing in the scent of the pine and moss. It was so beautiful up here, so peaceful. He and Rylee had spent a lot of time wandering these woods in the summers. Maybe not as much time as they'd spent at the movies and at the river, but a fair amount. They'd come up here when it was hot in town, and when they'd had too much sun and water, and they'd sit in the meadow grass and talk. They'd had some of their best talks up here, with the stars just beginning to pierce the evening sky and the moon lifting its pale face in the east. Shep coveted those long-lost moments. And he coveted this place.

Slowing, he touched her elbow then came to a stop on the trail. The mountain air was cool against his skin. Birds and squirrels rustled in the bushes to their left, and the sun was trying its best to peek through the steely blanket of clouds overhead. Overall, this spot hadn't changed at all since he and Rylee had hung out here as kids. It was untouched by time, and Shep knew what a rarity that was in this day and age.

He turned to his right, to the meadow that was visible now through the trees. The grass, deep green from the recent spring rains, was punctuated by fragrant wildflowers that moved in the breeze. Even though the air still held a chill, the warmth in the sunshine carried a hint of the seasonal change on the way. It was a perfect afternoon as far as he was concerned. A perfect place, with perfect company.

He let his gaze settle on the aspen tree closest to them. The one with the large knot in its trunk about halfway up. It was the first one you came to when walking along this trail. The first one in the grove surrounding the meadow. And he'd carved something into it a long, long time ago. When he'd been a kid, and when his best friend had meant more to him than just about anyone else in the world.

"Rylee," he said.

She turned, her cheeks flushed and her eyes bright. He could smell the faint scent of her perfume mixed in with the sweet smell of the wildflowers and grass. Her lips were full and pink and glistening, and she looked so pretty right then that she just about killed him dead.

He reached for her, and she put her hand in his. He just hoped he wouldn't screw this up, like he'd screwed up so many other things lately.

"I wanted to bring you here," he said, "because it's always been a special place for me."

She smiled. "Me, too."

"I know we've talked about our childhoods and the things that were hard for us. But I'm not sure you ever knew how worried I was that I'd end up like my dad."

She watched him, her eyes full of understanding. He was lucky to have a friend like Rylee. Sometimes he wondered if she knew him better than he knew himself. Having a person like that in your life was special. It made him feel like he had everything to lose. And maybe everything to gain.

"He's changed," he continued. "He's gotten better with age, and he finally grew up. But for a long time, he made my mom miserable. He made our entire family miserable, and I never wanted to be like that. But when I was a kid, I thought it was a foregone conclusion. I refused to imagine myself married in the future, or even in a relationship that mattered, because it always made me so unsettled to picture that kind of life. Where I could have such a negative effect on other people. People who loved me, and who I loved back. After a while, I stopped thinking about it consciously. It just...*was*."

Rylee nodded, listening in that way that made him feel like he mattered. That he was important. That he was loved. It gave him the courage to pull her closer, until he could feel the softness of her body next to his. She fit perfectly there, making him think about those negative expectations that had always been a part of his narrative. Making him think about what it would be like to finally say goodbye to them, once and for all. He thought it would probably be a wonderful feeling, changing and growing like that. And he knew Rylee was the only woman he'd be able to make that change for.

"That's why I left the morning after we slept together," he said quietly. "It was just easier than facing this dumb fear that I've always had. Can you forgive me? For leaving you like I did?"

She reached up and touched his face. The tips of her fingers left his skin tingling. They left his heart tingling.

"I can't believe you've ever been scared of anything," she said. "To me, you've always been fearless. But you telling me this... I have to be honest. It makes me love you even more, Shep. And that scares *me*. Because I didn't think I could love you any more than I already did."

He laughed. "Well, then. I think this might be the perfect time to show you what I brought you up here for."

"It's not the meadow?"

"No. Look."

He pointed to the aspen tree next to them. The one with the knot in its trunk. Below the knot was a heart carved into the snow-white bark. And inside the heart was another carving. *S+R*.

Rylee gasped. "Did you…"

"I carved that when I was ten. Back when I thought just about anything was possible. Before I got jaded by things."

She stared at it. "Shep…"

"So, you see," he said, leaning down to kiss her temple, careful to be gentle with the cut there, "I think I've always loved you, too."

She smiled, looking happier than he'd ever seen her. But the wariness was there, too. And she had every right to be wary of him. He was wary of himself. But something was different now. He could feel it.

"I don't know," she said, her voice low. "Do you think something could work between us? Do you think we should start dating?"

Shep wrapped his arms around her waist. They were good together. They'd always been good together. Maybe this was what people meant when they talked about fate. Suddenly, that old fear he'd battled for so long began receding as he stood there with her in his arms. As he clearly pictured them in the future. Together. Happy. It was something he never thought would be in the cards for him, but that was the thing with change. True change. It could take you by surprise in the best possible ways.

"You want me to be honest with you?" he asked. "Really honest?"

"You know I do."

"Then I have to say I don't want to date you, Rylee."

Her expression fell. Her body stiffened. But before she could pull away, he held her fast.

"I want to marry you," he finished softly. "I don't want to be your boyfriend. I want to be your husband."

She stared up at him. "You want to get married," she repeated. "For real…"

He nodded. Then leaned down and kissed her on the lips. Tasting her. Loving her. When he pulled away, her eyes were red-rimmed and glassy.

"I'm just sorry it took me this long," he said, "to see what I had in front of me this whole time."

Swallowing visibly, she reached up and wrapped her arms around his neck. She was shaking. He could feel it.

"Maybe we just needed a little push," she said. "I'm not sure I would've had the courage without one. And then there was the necklace…"

"The necklace?"

She smiled. "Maybe that was the little push. Fate or magic. Or whatever you want to call it." She told him then, about what the mayor had said about the necklace's power.

"I like that. Magic." He spread his hand over her lower back, rubbing his thumb against the sliver of skin above her jeans. "And all before we turn thirty."

"Just in the nick of time."

"So…" He looked down into her clear blue eyes. "Does this mean you're saying yes?"

"Are you asking me to marry you, Shep Dalton?"

"I am. I'm asking you to marry me. Except I don't have

a ring. Again." He laughed. "I guess you'll have to trust me on that part."

"It's a leap of faith."

"Will you take it with me?"

The sound of the forest enveloped them like a hug. Their aspen tree shivered in the breeze. Pretty soon, it would be alive with leaves that would turn red and gold in the fall. But for the summer months ahead, they would be as green as the swimming hole he and Rylee had shared as kids. As the river that had always led them home again. They'd grown up in two very different families, but they were the same in so many ways. Those similarities had brought them back together again. And yeah, Shep thought, maybe that was magic. Maybe it was fate. Whatever it was, he was grateful it had touched his life like it had. And had brought Rylee with it.

Her smile widened, and it was like the sun coming out from behind the clouds. Until right then, he hadn't realized how worried he was that she'd say no. They'd had a rocky start with this whole marriage thing, after all. And it was fast. Some might say lightning fast. But if you considered the fact that they'd known each other, and loved each other, since elementary school, then it really wasn't fast at all.

She stood on her tiptoes and kissed him softly. Sweetly. "I will," she said. "I absolutely will."

Rylee stood in front of the giant living-room window and looked out over the lush green expanse of Dalton's Grange. Today was one of those late spring Montana days that was so rare she wanted to stop time altogether, just so she could sit in the sun and soak as much of it up as possible. Days like this got her through the long winters, when it seemed like the snow would never stop falling and the wind would never stop howling. But they always did. Spring always came. And with it, days like this. Full of warmth and hope and promises of the future.

Footsteps approached behind her—boots thudding on the hardwood floor. She knew it was Shep long before he wrapped his arms around her waist and moved her hair aside to kiss her neck. Lately, it seemed like she could sense his presence before he'd even entered the room. It was like he was a part of her. And she was a part of him.

"What are you doing?" he asked, his mouth close to her ear.

Everyone was talking and laughing across the room. Enjoying the party and the food and the company. They'd come to celebrate Shep's thirtieth birthday, but he seemed to be more focused on Rylee than anything else. Not that she was complaining. She could get used to this kind of attention.

"Just thinking," she said, turning her face into his.

"About?"

"About how we got here."

"To the party?"

She laughed. "To this point in our lives. How funny it is that it all ended up like this."

"Engaged."

She nodded.

"I think it makes perfect sense," he said evenly. "It was meant to be."

It was one of his favorite things to say now. That they were meant to be. And she couldn't argue. She agreed with all her heart. But sometimes, she couldn't understand how she'd gotten so lucky. She felt like the luckiest woman in the world, and that still felt delicate. Like it all might come tumbling down again if she wasn't careful.

But whenever she thought about it that way, whenever she felt the fear taking over, she remembered what Shep had said in their meadow a few weeks ago. He'd asked her to trust him. And that was exactly what she intended to do. She loved him. And that meant putting her faith into this relationship. As new and tender as it was. If they could both do that, put their faith into it, it would grow into something special. Even more special than it already was. Like that pearl necklace that she thought about all the time now, it would grow into something magical.

He kissed her cheek, and she closed her eyes, reveling in the feel of his lips on her skin. How his stubble scraped against it, and how his breath was warm in her ear. She loved Shep with her whole heart. And every time she thought about becoming his wife, she wanted to pinch herself all over again. It was her childhood fantasy coming true. The sweetest promise being kept.

"I think I'm supposed to say something before my mom cuts the cake," he said.

"That cake looks amazing."

"It does, doesn't it? When you turn thirty, everyone gets excited about things like cake. Including the birthday boy." He winked at her. "You'll see when it's your turn."

"I know. I'm right behind you."

"Only a few more weeks and you'll be entering another decade, baby."

"At least you're blazing the trail for me."

"That I am."

"Shep! It's time, honey!" Deborah called from across the room. Her voice carried over the country music playing on the stereo. She was so happy to be giving Shep this party. Even happier that Rylee was here to help him celebrate. She'd told her over and over again. It was nice for Rylee to feel like she belonged here. Like she was already family.

Before leaving Tenacity, she'd told her parents that her and Shep's engagement was officially back on. She could tell they were still worried it might be too fast. Her dad was especially hesitant about it, and she could understand that. It took a lot for him to come around to most things. She just hoped they'd feel more comfortable with it soon, since Gabby, as the maid of honor, was on fire to make an appointment at Ever After to try on dresses. Her mother had promised to drive up to Bronco for that. Rylee wouldn't have it any other way.

Shifting, she laid her head on Shep's chest and gazed out at all the people in the room. All of Shep's family and friends were there, along with townspeople from Bronco. Gabby was there, with Ryan and Bella, and so were Rylee's parents. Even Winona Cobbs and her fiancé, Stanley Sanchez, were there. Winona and Stanley were finally getting married in July. Some people didn't think they'd ever get around to making it official, but July was just around the corner, and they looked pretty happy as far as Rylee could tell.

It was a good turnout. A lot of people loved Shep. But she didn't think anyone could love him more than she did. For the first time in a very long time, she was looking forward to her future, and all the unknowns that might come with it. Because if she was facing it with Shep, she knew they could make an adventure out of just about anything. Even the hardest days.

He gave her a squeeze and kissed the top of her head. "I'll be right back."

She watched him make his way across the room—handsome, broad-shouldered, confident, sexy. *Her Shep.*

Gabby walked over and elbowed her gently in the ribs. "You're glowing, girlfriend."

"I am?"

"You absolutely are. I don't think I've ever seen you this happy, Rylee."

So, it showed. But she guessed that made sense. Everything felt so close to the surface lately. Like it had just been waiting to rise to the top. The happiness, the joy. The love.

Gabby put an arm around her as they watched Shep step onto a stool and lift a champagne glass in the air. He tapped it with a fork, and a hush fell over the room.

"I think he's your destiny," Gabby whispered. "And that's pretty romantic."

Rylee smiled, her gaze resting on the handsome cowboy who had stolen her heart all those years ago. And had kept it tucked in his pocket ever since. It belonged to him, she thought. And it always would.

"Thank you all for coming," he said. "Thirty years old today. *Ouch.*"

Everyone laughed.

"When I was younger," he continued, "and when I thought about this day, the only thing I knew for sure was that I didn't want to celebrate it without my best friend by my side. And now, I can happily say that she is. Because she's not only my best friend, but also my fiancée. It's been a little bit of a learning curve for us, but I can't imagine spending the rest of my life with anyone else. Rylee, would you come up here for a minute? I have something for you."

Rylee stared at him. Gabby gave her a little push, until she finally stepped forward through the throng of people and up to where Shep was standing.

He stepped off the stool and grinned down at her. Playful, mischievous Shep. Always keeping her on her toes. Always keeping her young at heart. When he looked at her like this, anything was possible.

"I should've given this to you weeks ago," he said.

He took her hand and placed something in her palm. Something cool and tiny. She looked down at it and felt her heart skip a beat. It was a ring. A beautiful antique ring that immediately took her breath away.

"It was my grandmother's," he said. "She would've loved you, honey."

There was a collective *aww* that moved through the room as Rylee felt people craning their necks, trying to get a glimpse.

With her heart thumping in her ears, she slipped the ring onto her finger and held it up to the light. The diamonds glittered like stars, the white-gold band glinting in the sunlight coming through the window. She didn't think she'd ever seen anything so lovely in her life. It was exactly what she would've chosen for herself. Exactly.

She turned to Shep with a terrible ache in her throat. For a second, she worried she wouldn't be able to speak. To tell him how much she loved the ring and how much she loved him. How excited she was to become his wife. But then, she didn't have to.

Slowly, he took her in his arms and leaned down to kiss her.

The room erupted in applause, and she felt herself being lifted off the ground. Her feet dangled in the air as he held her against his chest. She felt laughter bubble up from the deepest parts of her. It was the same feeling she'd had when they'd held hands and jumped off the rock into their swimming hole. The same feeling she'd had when they'd stood in his driveway the day she'd left for college, when they'd made their promise to each other. It was a feeling of weightlessness. Of pure, unrelenting joy.

When he set her down again, people made their way forward to congratulate them. Her parents, smiling and happy. His parents, looking proud of them both. Their friends and family. And then Winona Cobbs, in a flowy white dress and chunky costume jewelry that sparkled in the afternoon light. Even in her nineties, she was still a very beautiful woman, and Rylee found herself looking down at her in wonder. She knew some people in town thought she was eccentric, maybe even a little nutty, but Rylee had always thought she was wise. She'd seen so much in her lifetime. She had so much to share.

"Congratulations, sweetheart," Winona said with a smile. Her soft, powdery wrinkles deepened then. Her cheeks were flushed pink, and she wore an understated lipstick that reminded Rylee of roses.

"Thanks so much, Winona."

Shep took her thin, delicate hand and kissed her knuckles, just like Prince Charming. "I'm so glad you could make it," he said.

She smiled wider, obviously taken with his charm, just like everyone else. "I wouldn't miss it, Shep. We get to celebrate your birthday *and* your new life with this lovely girl."

Rylee leaned into Shep's side, and he put his arm around her waist. They stood there with Winona, who suddenly looked wistful.

"Being young and in love is a wonderful thing," the older woman said. "Josiah and I...well, it's a long story, meant for some other day..."

Rylee watched her. A curious expression crossed the older woman's face, just as the music changed to something slower and softer. When Winona had been a young woman, she'd had quite the secret romance with a rancher named Josiah Abernathy. Most everyone in Bronco knew about it now, but there was still an air of mystery surrounding their love affair, even all these years later. Rylee would love to hear the story if Winona ever decided to tell it.

She reached out and touched Winona's arm. The other woman jumped a little, as if startled from her thoughts.

"Are you okay?" Rylee asked.

"Oh, I'm fine, sweetie. Just taking a trip down memory lane." She glanced behind her at Stanley, who was helping himself to a piece of cake. She frowned, and Rylee thought some of the cheerful color had drained from her face. But maybe that was just her imagination.

"Well," Winona said, turning back to them again. "You two enjoy the party. Happiest of birthdays to you, Shep."

Rylee watched her go, her billowy white dress making her stand out like an exclamation point in the room full of Wranglers and plaid shirts.

"Now, there goes a very interesting woman," Shep said, pulling Rylee close.

"You can say that again. She has a lot of secrets."

"Yes, she does."

Rylee turned to Shep and tilted her head back to look up into his handsome face.

"You're thirty today," she said.

"That, I am."

"I'll be thirty in just a few weeks."

"Indeed."

"And we're getting married." Her voice caught in her throat. She felt such naked emotion right then that it probably should have embarrassed her. But she didn't care. She wanted him to know. She wanted him to know everything that lay in her heart.

He cupped her face in both hands. Then he moved his thumbs across her cheekbones and leaned down to kiss her lightly on the lips.

"We're getting married," he murmured against her mouth.

"Is it too soon to make another promise?"

He smiled. "Never. What is it?"

"Promise we'll always be together."

Rylee was a realist. She knew life would throw things at them that they weren't prepared for. Or that might change their existence forever. Things that weren't anyone's fault, they just *were*. So maybe it wasn't fair to ask for that. But deep down, she knew that Shep would know what she meant.

She wanted to know that they'd always love each other. No matter what. No matter what might happen in the future. Whether they could control those things or not. She wanted to know that their love would transcend time and space. That it would transcend circumstance and just *be*. Like the color of the river in the summer or the scent of their meadow in the spring. It would always be.

"That," Shep said softly against her ear, so only she could hear, "is a promise I can keep."

* * * * *

Look for the next installment in the new continuity
Montana Mavericks: The Anniversary Gift

The Maverick's Thirty-Day Marriage
by Rochelle Alers

On sale May 2024,
wherever Harlequin books
and ebooks are sold.

And don't miss
Sweet-Talkin' Maverick
by Christy Jeffries

Maverick's Secret Daughter
by USA TODAY *bestselling*
author Catherine Mann

Available now!